# GUN BLAZE VALLEY

The Mimbres Valley was quiet and peaceful until someone decided he wanted a change. Then things started happening. Indians left the reservation and went on the warpath. A man was found with a knife in his back. Another was found hanging from his window. There was only one man left who could stop the terror—and that was Bob Nevins. But even his blazing six-gun couldn't help him shoot his way out of a frame-up.

# GUN BLAZE VALLEY

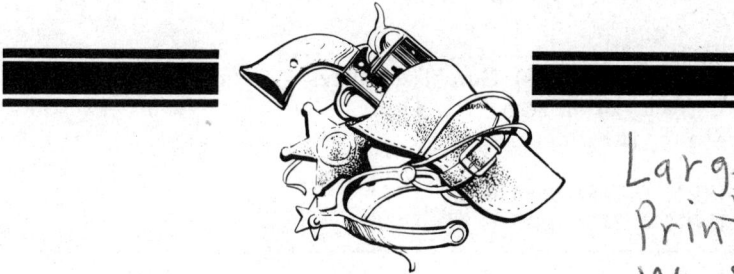

## Charles Alden Seltzer

## ATLANTIC LARGE PRINT
Chivers Press, Bath, England.
Curley Publishing, Inc.,
South Yarmouth, Mass., USA.

Library of Congress Cataloging-in-Publication Data

Seltzer, Charles Alden, 1875–1942.
  Gunblaze Valley / Charles Alden Seltzer.
      p.  cm.—(Atlantic large print)
  ISBN 0–7927–0070–8 (soft: lg. print)
  1. Large type books.  I. Title.  II. Title: Gun Blaze Valley.
[PS3537.E4G85  1990]
813'.52—dc20                                        89–23428
                                                         CIP

British Library Cataloguing in Publication Data

Seltzer, Charles Alden
    [Valley of the stars]. Gun blaze valley.—(Atlantic large print).
    I. [Valley of the stars]   II. Title
    813'.52 [F]


    ISBN 0–7451–9664–0
    ISBN 0–7451–9675–6

This Large Print edition is published by Chivers Press, England, and
Curley Publishing, Inc, U.S.A. 1990

Published by arrangement with Donald MacCampbell Inc

U.K. Hardback  ISBN  0 7451 9664 0
U.K. Softback  ISBN  0 7451 9675 6
U.S.A. Softback  ISBN  0 7927 0070 8

# CHAPTER ONE

Mr. Robert M. Nevins did not appear at Deming for two days after he was to meet Edna Pendleton and Hale Seaton. Edna was to assume a partnership in a Mimbres Valley Ranch, with the aid of her legal advisor, Seaton. Miss Pendleton had personally spoken to Gibson, the proprietor of the hotel, about Mr. Nevins, but the lank gentleman had given her no hope. Instead, he had curiously squinted his eyes at her as she talked.

'Nevins is an odd cuss,' he said. 'You sure you ain't got your dates mixed?'

'We advised him that we would arrive here on the morning of the sixteenth of April. He answered that he would meet us here. This is the seventeenth.'

'It sure is. Wa-al, I wouldn't worry none. Give him time. It's likely he'll show up.' He glanced at a clock on the wall, whose hands pointed to three. 'The day ain't over yet,' he added.

Miss Pendleton asked Gibson to notify her when Nevins came; then she walked out to the dusty veranda and seated herself in a chair. Disdaining the chairs, Seaton leaned against one of the veranda columns, sullenly regarding the country.

From where she sat Miss Pendleton could see many miles into the northern distance, but in all the vast expanse of land she could detect no sign of movement.

Seaton followed her gaze. The low, silent hills, most of them black and featureless; the vast stretches of desolate plain between; the strange, strained stillness, seemed to oppress Seaton.

'Beastly country!' he declared.

'Yes,' answered Edna; 'it is. But, Hale, do you see that space between those hills? Look how the sun shines down upon it. Why, it looks level as a floor! It would be wonderful to ride out there. There are miles upon miles of level land that one could easily get lost in.'

'I've no desire to get lost,' said Seaton. 'And I like a country with more scenery in it. There's nothing here that's at all picturesque.'

Miss Pendleton flashed a glance at Seaton. She did not reply to him, but sat very still, looking at a sky which had become turquoise, and which was flecked with clouds as white as fleece. Never in her life had Miss Pendleton seen colors as pure and vivid as those at which she now gazed. And the land, lying calm and serene, was as restful to her eyes as a rich mural painting in fresh tints viewed from cool shadows.

She was strangely stirred, and she wondered if she had not inherited something

2

of her father's admiration for this country. He had lived in the West for many years before moving back to New York and his buying of a share in a ranch in southern New Mexico had been a phase of his love for the region.

She strongly suspected that Seaton's disgust of the country was based upon fear of it. Living here would mean contact with the primitive, with all the discomforts and the inconveniences one inevitably met in a new, unsettled country.

Mr. Nevins did not appear. The afternoon waned and the dusk came. It stole over the land solemnly, bringing a strange, weird hush. The town seemed to huddle under it, to shrink and shrivel from the awful majesty of it.

No Eastern dusk had ever been like this. In the East the dusk came prosaically, naturally. One never marveled at it. But out here it settled like a pall; it was impalpable, mysterious, monstrous.

Seaton seemed to dislike the dusk. He had gone inside the hotel when the shadows first began to fall. Miss Pendleton saw him sitting in one of the dusty chairs in the lobby, moodily smoking. He had his back turned toward the veranda.

The girl stepped from the veranda edge and made her way down the dark street. After a while she came to an open space that appeared to stretch between some buildings.

3

She saw the cold, brilliant points of stars twinkling in a soft, velvety blue sky, and she stood for some time watching them. She had never seen more stars, nor brighter ones.

She stood there long, meditating. And then a voice reached her ears. It appeared to come from a point very close to her; she felt that she was so near that had she so desired she might have reached out and touched the speaker. It was Ross's voice, a cowboy she had seen at the hotel during the day. It startled her into trembling rigidity.

'You'll have to be the judge of that, Fagin!' he said.

The voice was cold, level, passionless.

It came smoothly and quietly, and yet Miss Pendleton seemed to feel that the atmosphere around her had suddenly chilled. The voice which answered was cool, mocking.

'I've been judgin' my actions for a right smart while. I don't need to ask anybody to do any judgin' for me. That's why I sprung this on you. You've been havin' opinions—an' airin' them.'

'You mean I have been sayin' things about you? You are wrong, Fagin. You know I never say anything about a man unless I'm sure. An', as I told you, I ain't sure about that Two Diamond cow.'

'Wade Hull says you mentioned it to him.'

'I wasn't mentionin' any names, Fagin.'

It seemed to Miss Pendleton that she could

4

feel the man called 'Fagin' squirm. There was a rasp of rage in his voice when he replied:

'No, no names. You didn't mention any. But the way you spoke led Wade Hull to think you was talkin' about me an' Adams. There's never been any love between you an' me, Ross. I ain't admirin' you none!'

'We're even there, Fagin. But I don't want any trouble with you.'

'You've never wanted it,' sneered Fagin. 'But if you don't close your mouth I'll close it for you!'

'Right now,' said Ross; 'if you ain't talkin' through your hat!'

There came another silence. Evidently Fagin was 'talking through his hat,' or discretion was calming his rage. The silence continued for so long a time that Miss Pendleton felt the men must overhear her labored breathing. For she was certain tragedy would follow Ross's words. She almost screamed with relief when Fagin's voice finally came.

'I ain't aimin' to do nothin' until I'm certain,' he said. 'But if I hear any more talk—' The unfinished sentence carried a sinister threat.

Ross laughed. 'I won't be hard to find if you come lookin' for me,' he declared. 'But I'm tellin' you one thing, Fagin: if you an' Brandt Adams figure to stay in this country an' keep healthy, you want to keep a considerable distance away from the Circle Dot range!'

'We'll use our judgment about that,' said Fagin.

Miss Pendleton heard a step, and surmised that Fagin had taken himself off. She stood silent, waiting for Ross to move. Then she heard another sound, a mere rustle. And she felt a hard object pressing between her shoulder-blades.

She was certain the object was the muzzle of a revolver, and her knees sagged in fright. While she stood, powerless to move, a hand touched her shoulder and slid lightly down her arm.

'A woman!' came Ross's voice. 'Thought it was Brandt Adams, tryin' to pot-shot me! What in blazes are you doin' here?'

Reaction from her fright brought on a cold rage.

'That is none of your business!' she declared. 'Please remove your hand!'

'When you have been here a little while you'll know better than to be out alone at night,' he advised.

'I shall go wherever I please and whenever I please!' she announced.

'I reckon you will,' he conceded.

Miss Pendleton did not reply. There was something about the man that irritated her to a fury.

6

# CHAPTER TWO

'No,' said Gibson, the proprietor of the hotel, 'Bob Nevins didn't come in last night. Nor I ain't seen no sign of anybody ridin' the north trail this mornin', though I've been watchin', sort of expectin' him. It's likely he's forgot you. Or mebbe somethin''s happened to him. Nobody can't ever tell anything about Bob Nevins.'

Miss Pendleton's lips straightened with decision.

'Then we'll have to go on without him,' she declared. 'I presume we shall have to have a guide. Do you know one you could recommend?'

Gibson scratched his chin and gazed out into the brilliant morning sunshine. She followed his gaze. It seemed to her that there had come a change in the appearance of the country since yesterday. The pass through the hills northward appeared lonely and dismal; desolation sat on the bare ridges; menace seemed to crouch in the valleys. An eighty-mile ride!

'There ain't no one that I can think of right now,' said Gibson. 'All the boys that hit town last night has pulled their freight. An' there ain't none of the boys which live in town that would be worth their salt guidin' anybody in that country.'

Gibson appeared depressed at not being able to serve his guests. 'Shucks!' he exclaimed; 'usually there's somebody. Just you an' your friend set down there a minute while I think. No; you don't need to. Say, ain't I a box-head? There's Ross! Sure! He told me last night that he was lightin' out this mornin'! You just follow his trail an' he'll take you through without any fuss at all!'

'Ross,' said Miss Pendleton, without enthusiasm. Her chin went up. 'Really,' she said coldly, 'we couldn't think of inconveniencing Mr. Ross.'

'Not a darned bit of incon—convenience!' declared Gibson. 'Ross will be blamed glad to have comp'ny. He's the darndest cuss that way you ever seen!'

'I think we could dispense with Mr. Ross if we could find some other person,' Seaton suggested. 'If you should ask me, I believe Mr. Ross is a rather—er—reckless character.'

'Wa-al, I ain't never heard anybody say that Ross is reckless,' Gibson said, judicially cocking his head to one side. 'There's folks that say Ross is a little set in his ways an' kind of hard to handle in a fuss; but if I was lookin' for a guide which had plain common sense an' a knack of gettin' out of trouble with a whole skin, I wouldn't look no further than Ross.'

'Would there be any prospect of another

8

guide appearing shortly, Mr. Gibson?' Miss Pendleton wanted to know.

'That's hard to tell,' said Gibson. 'Might be somebody ride in tomorrow who knows that section. An' then again, it might be a month or so. But there ain't no need of waitin', far as I can see. Jim Gideon will rent you a couple of hosses an' you can light out without any guide.'

Miss Pendleton betrayed no enthusiasm at the suggestion. She looked at Seaton, nibbled her lips, and gazed into the northern distance.

'We'll engage Mr. Ross,' she decided.

'That's sensible!' declared Gibson. 'I seen him down to the blacksmith shop a while ago. I'll go an' tell him to get the hosses ready.'

An hour later, when Ross rode up to the hotel, leading two horses, Miss Pendleton and Seaton were sitting on the veranda waiting for him. She gave Ross a short nod of recognition; Seaton sullenly gazed past him, affecting not to see him.

Ross did not dismount. The tall, lank man sat motionless in the saddle, gazing straight ahead, while Miss Pendleton was helped upon the back of one of the horses by Seaton. Then Seaton mounted.

Still Ross did not turn. He sat there in apparent indifference to what was going on behind him, until Miss Pendleton spoke impatiently:

'Well, we are ready!'

9

Ross urged his horse northward. Seaton followed him closely, while Miss Pendleton rode at a little distance behind.

They had no more than left Deming's one street when the wild, virgin land engulfed them. Half an hour later, following a turn and a descent, they were in a dry gulch that hemmed in the heat and seemed to draw the rays of the sun straight down upon them.

The land descended gradually and the heat grew more oppressive. Seaton began to complain, but Ross paid no attention to him, riding steadily forward, not looking back.

Watching both Seaton and Ross, Miss Pendleton was amazed at the contrast between them. Seaton was stouter than was good for him. His face was florid; he continually perspired and mopped the moisture with a handkerchief. He was visibly suffering from the heat.

Miss Pendleton was herself oppressed, and she envied Ross, who rode along steadily, apparently unmindful of the discomfort that was affecting his companions.

Once when they reached a washout, and Ross pulled up his horse on the other side and half turned in the saddle in apparent concern for their ability to negotiate the dangerous spot, Miss Pendleton spoke:

'It is unusually hot, isn't it?'

'Not unusually,' he answered. 'But April is an uncertain month. You might say it's variable. Heat an' coolness mingle. About next month the heat will begin to put in its best licks. By August, if you stay in this country that long, you'll be wantin' to shoot anybody who says anything to you about the weather.'

'I shall stay; but I don't expect to shoot anyone.'

Ross did no more talking. Apparently he had lost all interest in them. His attitude appeared to speak eloquently of total indifference.

They got out of a ravine into some mountains. Miss Pendleton discovered the level she had seen from Deming, but she was not to enjoy riding upon it, for they crossed only an edge of it when they began to descend into a big valley. It was not so hot here, but they were not to enjoy the valley as much as Miss Pendleton hoped, for they were no sooner in it than Ross urged his horse into a short, choppy gallop.

Seaton and Miss Pendleton fell far behind. Seaton continually complained, but she paid no attention to him, for she was experiencing a cold rage against Ross for his indifference. Also, she began to become apprehensive that Ross was deliberately drawing away from them with the malicious purpose of losing them. She saw him, far ahead, a mere speck on the dun-colored plain.

She wouldn't hurry; she'd not give him the

satisfaction of thinking she had to depend
that much upon him. He was a prig, after all,
and he was now betraying the character that
all along she had imputed to him. He was one
of those men of narrow mentality whose pose
was self-confidence and authority.

He hadn't any real ability or he would not
be a mere cowboy, living out here in a place
so desolate and remote and taking care of
cows for a living. A real man's place was in
the marts of trade or business. A profession
was, of course, quite beyond him.

But somehow her vindictive meditations
were unsatisfying. For one thing, the object
of them didn't know what they were, and,
judging from the indifference with which he
kept on increasing the distance between
himself and his charges, he didn't or
wouldn't, care if he knew.

She didn't urge her horse, nor did she draw
him in. She permitted him to travel along at
the gait he had chosen. And apparently the
animal had no intention of trying to keep up
with the horse Ross rode, for he continued to
fall behind until when noon came Ross was
nearly out of sight.

They kept going, and Miss Pendleton
began to think seriously of water. She wasn't
perspiring; she was baking, slowly shriveling.
She got a malicious satisfaction from
contemplating Seaton's misery. He appeared
almost ready to collapse. Then her thoughts

went again to Ross. She had to keep her teeth tightly pressed together or she would have anathematized them aloud.

She had ridden in front of Seaton, and now she rode on, rigid as possible in the saddle, indignant. When she finally caught up with Ross—if she did catch up with him—she meant to tell him a few things in no uncertain manner. She would convince him that she was no child, to be treated as he was treating her.

But when, after following the trail down a dry arroyo, she suddenly rounded a bend and came upon Ross stooping over a frying pan under which he had built a small fire of dry chaparral, she brought her horse to a halt and sat in the saddle, vacillating, uncertain. For the aroma of frying bacon assailed her nostrils. She realized that she was very hungry, and she believed that never in her life had the scent of food seemed so good.

Ross had built his fire in the center of a little flat at the edge of a narrow, shallow, sparkling clear stream of water. There was grass, some trees, shade. As Miss Pendleton sat in the saddle gazing with gratified eyes at the scene, she became aware of a slight, cool breeze. Somehow, her indignation lost some of its edge.

'Oh,' she said, 'you are here! I thought you had gone on.'

She was disappointed to realize that the

13

sarcasm she had meant to put into her voice appeared to be not sarcasm at all, but relief. Ross arose and faced her, frying pan in hand. She could hear the bacon sizzle; and the cloud of blue-white smoke that rose from the frying pan gave her a feeling of panic.

'You are burning it!' she warned.

Ross critically surveyed the contents of the pan.

'I reckon not,' he returned. 'I like it crisp.'

His hat was pushed back from his forehead, and Miss Pendleton observed that the brow was white, high, well shaped, and that some of the brown-black hair, pushed down by the hat-band, was in a moist, matted wave just above one eyebrow.

The recreant lock, gleaming in the sun, gave him a singularly negligent and wayward appearance; and a gleam in his eyes, which Miss Pendleton was certain could be nothing less than derision, convinced her that he wasn't much concerned about her opinions. In fact, so far as she could observe, he wasn't in the least affected by her arrival.

She waited, though, still half expecting him to be polite enough to offer to help her down, for he must have perceived that Seaton had not yet come in sight. But when he turned his back to her and continued to manipulate the frying pan, she frowned, got down without his assistance, and started toward him.

'Trail the reins!' he said shortly.

14

'What do you mean?'

She stood very erect, irritated by his tone.

'Throw the reins over his head,' he said. 'If you don't, he'll stray, an' when you want him you won't have him.'

She complied, meanwhile watching his back. He had not turned, and she wondered how he knew that she had not 'trailed' the reins when she had dismounted. Had he stolen a glance at her at that minute, or was he positive that in her ignorance of range-bred horses she was not aware that the reins must be trailed?

She stood for a little time, watching him. He went on frying the bacon, not looking at her. She made a face at him and walked to the edge of the stream, a little distance from the fire, and began to bathe her face with water that she scooped up in her hands.

Her ablutions did not appear to interest him, and while she dried her face with a handkerchief she studied his profile. She decided he would be good-looking if it weren't for the slightly cynical droop of his lips.

She moved a little closer and seated herself upon a boulder. He had set the frying pan down, and while she sat on the boulder, watching him, he took a coffee pot from a roll of tarpaulin that he had spread out near the fire, rinsed it in the stream, filled it with water and set it upon three small stones over

15

the fire. Then he stood up, stretched himself, and spoke, his back to her.

'Twenty-five miles,' he said.

So he was aware that she was within sound of his voice! She had thought from his manner that he didn't know, or care, if she was within a mile of him!

'What is twenty-five miles, please?' she asked coldly.

'The distance we've come. This is Buckner's Flat. It is where Captain Buckner and a company of his men were ambushed by Apaches. One man got out of that mess. The soldiers camped here and the Indians surprised them at night.' He pointed. 'Over there by that big rock they found Buckner. He'd been—'

'Oh!' she interrupted, 'please don't!'

'I wasn't goin' into details,' he said. 'It wasn't pretty.'

'Was that—er—recent?'

'Two years.'

'And have the Indians been punished?'

'Those Indians were. But it ain't a common thing. The sapheads in Washington don't recommend violence in dealin' with the Indian. But sometimes there's an officer out here who loses his haid. An' then there's some justice done.'

He stopped to replenish the fire, and she sat contemplating the silent hills that rimmed the flat. Almost she could visualize the

16

soldiers camped here, while in the darkness the Indians stole upon them. She stared at a cleft between some hills westward, and almost screamed when she saw movement there.

She quietly got up and moved toward the fire. She was at Ross's side, her skirts almost touching him, when he felt her presence and looked up at her. Instantly he stood up and peered at her, his gaze probing, curious.

'You've turned mighty pale,' he said. 'What's wrong?'

'I saw something move over there.'

'Where?'

She pointed, and he turned before she could stretch her arm out, grasped it, and forced it down to her side. He was so close to her that his body nearly touched hers, and she stared, fascinated by the cold, alert light in his eyes.

He grinned mirthlessly, with straight lips.

'It's bad business to do any pointin' out here,' he cautioned. 'Somebody might misunderstand. Now you go back an' set on that rock again. An' after you've been there a little while you can tell me where you saw that movement.'

'It is directly west, I think,' she explained. 'On the other side of that gully. There is a space between two hills. There is some shrubbery on the north side of the southerly hill. And some small trees; I think they are spruce. The hills are about two miles from

17

here.'

'Nearer ten miles,' he said. 'Distance out here will fool you a heap. An' what did you think you saw?'

'It wasn't distinct. It was a large animal. I had an impression that it was a horse. It seemed to sink into the side of the hill.'

'That was all, eh?'

'Yes.'

'A steer, I reckon. If you thought it was somethin' else, I expect you've got a lively imagination.'

Reassured, for her first thought had been of Indians, she sat watching him prepare dinner.

But he knew there would be no cattle beyond the gully. For in that direction, for many miles, there was no grass or water.


## CHAPTER THREE

The bacon was done, fried to a crisp, and had been removed from the frying pan and placed on a small tin. The coffee had boiled, and had been set aside. Its pleasant aroma permeated the surrounding atmosphere. Ross had produced soda biscuit from the roll of tarpaulin out of which he had got the coffee pot, the tin dishes, and the provisions for the meal.

But Seaton had not arrived.

Miss Pendleton was impatient, for she was hungry. Ross glanced at the dry arroyo through which Miss Pendleton had ridden when she had come upon him standing over the fire. His view was obstructed by a sharp bend in the walls of the arroyo.

'I reckon Mr. Seaton ain't used to ridin',' he observed. Quizzically he glanced at the food. 'It ain't good when it's cold,' he added.

'Don't wait for him if you are hungry,' advised Miss Pendleton.

'I ain't hungry,' he said. 'I reckon I'll go look for him.'

He strode to where he had picketed his horse, swung into the saddle, and rode out of sight into the arroyo.

Miss Pendleton knew he would not have to go far to be able to get a view of the back trail, but she was instantly afflicted with an odd lonesomeness, and walked to her horse and stood beside him for companionship. And as she stood there she gazed intently at the breach in the hills where she had observed movement.

There was no movement there now. All around her reigned a heavy, oppressive silence freighted with an unnamable menace. Her heart seemed to leap in thankfulness when she heard the slow beating of hoofs around the bend in the arroyo and saw Ross returning.

He was walking his horse; he appeared a

trifle pale, as though enraged, and his lips were tightly set. Behind him, at a little distance, came Seaton.

Seaton was on foot, leading his horse. The animal was limping badly, dangling its left foreleg.

Ross dismounted near Miss Pendleton. In reply to her question as to what had happened, he spoke evenly, although she could detect impatience or something stronger in his voice.

'A stone in the frog of his hoof,' he replied. 'It had been in there for hours, cuttin' an' burnin'.'

'Oh, that's too bad!' she exclaimed. 'And Mr. Seaton didn't notice it?'

'There's some things he don't notice,' said Ross. He turned away and walked to the fire, where he sat down and began to pour coffee into a tin cup. He motioned to her and stolidly began eating a biscuit while she drank from the tin cup he gave her.

She was sorry for Seaton. He had walked far, for he was covered with dust and about exhausted. Meeting Ross's eyes she asked coldly:

'Mr. Seaton may have some coffee, I suppose?'

'Tell him to help himself,' said Ross.

It seemed puerile of Ross to continue his absurd habit of talking to Seaton through her, and Miss Pendleton suppressed an impulse to

20

say so. But something in Ross's eyes cautioned her to forbear; she was convinced that his temper was on edge and that very little provocation would be needed to cause an explosion.

So she silently filled the tin cup and passed it to Seaton. Once when Seaton glared resentfully at Ross, Miss Pendleton frowned a warning at him. Thereafter, Seaton kept his gaze away from Ross.

They did not linger at the meal. Ross finished first and strode over to Seaton's horse. He examined the hoof, led the animal a little distance, then left it and stood, arms folded, staring westward.

Without a word to Miss Pendleton or Seaton after they had finished, Ross collected his cooking utensils and the tin cup and plate, washed them in the stream, rolled them in the slicker, strapped the slicker to the cantle of the saddle, and stood beside his horse.

Miss Pendleton and Seaton had moved to the shade of a tree a little distance down the stream.

'We'd better be draggin' it,' he called to them.

They went to their horses and mounted, Seaton helping Miss Pendleton.

Ross looked at Miss Pendleton.

'Tell him to keep comin' no matter how bad his horse limps. We'll try to get another horse for him after a while.'

21

This time Miss Pendleton seemed to detect in Ross's voice a note of malice, and now his addressing Seaton through her did not appear so childish. Seaton had made an enemy.

In the middle of the afternoon, when they halted at a small stream to water their horses, Ross sat a little apart, and Miss Pendleton observed him fingering the cartridges that studded the belt around his waist. Also, she saw him lift his rifle from its saddle sheath and examine it. He worked its mechanism, and when he turned and perceived that she was watching him he smiled gravely.

'Quail for supper, if there's any around,' he said.

Now for the first time Miss Pendleton realized what a ride of eighty miles meant. It meant, perhaps, that they would have to camp in the open, and that they would not reach their destination until the following day.

'Shall we have to camp out?' she asked.

'I've been hopin' not,' was his answer. 'There's a nester named Porter lives down here a piece. If we can get there we'll have a bunk.' He looked at Seaton's horse, then back at her. 'But you'll have to tell your friend to shake a leg.'

They started again and got out of the valley in which they had been riding the greater part of the afternoon. For several hours they rode along ridges and around the bases of small hills, and late in the afternoon they descended the slope of a basin. Near the center of the basin they rode into a pass through a series of ridges and entered a gorge where a narrow trail ran along the banks of a small stream.

Above, in the high country, there had been very little sound, and very little verdure. Down here birds incessantly chattered, and there was the solemn, weird rustling of leaves. Above was lifeless calm; down in the gorge there was life and movement.

They were forced to ride slowly, for Seaton's horse was gradually failing. Seaton himself was a negligent rider, although, perhaps, he was not to blame when the animal stepped into a crevice between two rocks, slipped, twisted, and fell. Riding a little in advance of Seaton, Miss Pendleton heard a sharp snap.

Ross rode back, his face grim, set. Miss Pendleton could tell from the expression of his eyes that tragedy had come upon them. The horse was lying upon his side, moaning in a way which was almost human. Seaton had saved himself from injury by slipping out of the saddle when the horse fell, for the beast had gone down slowly.

Ross stood for an instant gazing down at the horse. Then he turned.

'Miss Pendleton,' he said, 'you are to get on my horse. Tell Mr. Seaton to take yours. You will ride on a little distance. I'll be right

23

after you.'

Miss Pendleton changed horses. Seaton clambered upon the one she had discarded. They rode on until a turn in the trail took them out of sight of Ross, where they halted.

Miss Pendleton held the tips of her fingers against her ear drums; Seaton sat dejectedly, waiting. There was one shot, which reverberated into a thousand echoes. Then followed a stillness, a monstrous hush.

Then Miss Pendleton felt movement, and Ross swung upon the saddle behind her. She said no word to him; sat motionless while he took the reins from her and sent the horse forward.

Strangely, as they rode with the shadows deepening around them, Miss Pendleton discovered that although she didn't like Ross she was glad to have him so close to her. He was protection that she felt she needed, although she couldn't have told why.

There was no visible menace; outwardly the flanking woods presented the appearance they had presented all afternoon. They had grown slightly denser in appearance, to be sure, since the sun had finally vanished from view and twilight was stealing over the world; and yet she felt that danger lurked in them.

Several times between sundown and the time when twilight began perceptibly to change to darkness, Ross halted his horse and sat motionless, listening. Miss Pendleton wondered what sound he sought. She could hear none that was foreign, none that she had not heard during the afternoon, except one which might have been the distant booming of a loon or the nearer crooning of a dove.

That sound she had been hearing frequently since the coming of twilight. Each time she had heard it a shiver had run through her. But always, back East, the sound had strangely affected her. To her it had never brought on a presentiment of evil.

Once when Ross halted the animal under them, she spoke to him without turning her head:

'Shall we reach your nester's cabin before dark?'

'I reckon not,' answered Ross. 'I figured your friend could make better time. Soon we'll have to camp.'

'Have you ridden this trail after dark?'

'It ain't done.' He drew a deep breath. 'It would have been the same goin' back,' he added.

'What would?'

He started, laughing softly.

'Was I talkin'?' he asked. 'Well, don't pay any attention to me. I'm one of them box-haids that sometimes does his thinkin' out loud. But I reckon that just now I wasn't thinkin'. Just figurin'.'

They were now riding the trail, which was only just visible.

25

'Thinking what?' she asked. For now in some way she felt his thoughts were very important. It was strange what a feeling had come over her.

Ross, it appeared to her, was searching for something he could not find in the darkness which had fallen. He rode slowly, peering into clefts and hollows and into places that appeared to be coverts. She wondered whether he could see anything, for the darkness had grown so dense that it was as if they were riding under a blanket which had shut out sky and stars.

Only a deeper blackness, or a seeming lessening of the black pressure that she felt around her, apprised her of open spaces they passed, into which Ross peered. She knew he was searching for something, for now and then she could feel him turn.

Seaton was close behind. At times Miss Pendleton could hear the breathing of his horse at the withers of the one she and Ross rode.

After a while Ross again brought his horse to a halt.

'I reckon we'll camp here,' he said. 'If it's just the same to you, I'd rather you and your friend didn't do any talkin'. Just listen an' do as you are told.'

'Certainly,' she whispered.

'Hold tight,' came his voice in her ear; 'we're goin' down a sharp slope. Seaton,' he added in the same low tone, 'you follow close behind.'

The horse wheeled at an acute angle, and instantly the saddle dipped under Miss Pendleton. She grimly held to the high pommel and forbore to scream when she had a sickening sensation of falling.

But she did not fall, and they continued to go sharply downward for an interminable distance. The horse went slowly, gingerly, picking his way carefully in the darkness, and Miss Pendleton was convinced that the animal had made this descent before.

When far down they struck a level, they stopped. Miss Pendleton could hear Seaton's horse coming. It reached a point beside them and halted.

Ross dismounted. He stood beside the horse and groped for Miss Pendleton's hand. When he found it he helped her down. Whispering to Seaton to follow, he led them away into the darkness.

Miss Pendleton had caught Seaton's arm, and the latter kept close. They now went upward, on a slope that at times became almost precipitous, and when, after five minutes had passed, Ross paused as if listening, Miss Pendleton whispered the fear that had gripped her all afternoon:

'Indians?'

'Yep.' There was a grimness in his voice. 'Their hootin' is a heap more silly now,' he added. 'They're fussin' around like a calf with hysterics.' He spoke with contempt. 'They expected us to keep right on ridin' until we got to a level up hereaways. Then they'd rope us. They're some disturbed that we haven't kept right on comin'. Pretty soon they'll come back, lookin' for us.'

'How many?' she whispered, her voice as low as his.

'Not many. A peace party, I reckon,' he said, his voice now derisive. 'They let them go that way visitin'. An' once they're off the reservation they quit bein' peaceful. But the fools at Washington don't know that, an' they keep on lettin' them go.'

'There may be a great many of them,' she said, dismayed.

'Not so many. Five or six, maybe. I've been noticin' their hootin'. If you listen you can just about tell where they are. Right now they're sneakin' around, tryin' to find out where we left the trail. You an' your friend slip through this brush. You'll be out of sight until daylight. There's an overhang here, with a hollow under it. You'll be mighty safe while it stays dark. An' if the thing lasts till daylight I'll be where I can cover this place with my rifle.'

'You are going to leave us?' She could not keep the dismay out of her voice.

'I'm hopin' not. I've got to get down where I can keep an eye on the horses. That's what

28

they'll be huntin' at first. Don't you make any noise, whatever you hear. An' don't come out from behind that brush.'

She felt his hand on her arm; heard some bushes crackle softly; some thorns grasped raspingly at her dress. And then she and Seaton were standing against a rocky wall. She whispered Ross's name, but there came no answer, no sound. Noiselessly he had slipped away.

She and Seaton stood under the rocky overhang, listening. From various points around them came a musical medley of forest voices: the croaking of tree toads, sustained, insistent; the chirping of crickets, shrill, incessant; the distant howling bark of a coyote; the hooting of owls.

Miss Pendleton paid little attention to the lower sounds, for her ears were attuned to the hooting of the owls, for in that sound was menace. She heard them all around her.

At first they were distant, but as time passed she became aware that the hooting was coming nearer. And when at last there came a low call so close to her that she could plainly hear the human note in it, she pressed her hands over her lips to suppress the scream that leaped to them.

# CHAPTER FOUR

After leaving Miss Pendleton and Seaton, Ross sank swiftly down the slope to the bottom of the cañon, where he had left the horses. He knew that there was little time, for far in the east was a mellow glow which foretold the rising of the moon.

While the hooting of the owls was still distant he reached the horses. He led them deep into a recess where there was a level sandy floor and a wild growth of timber and brush arching overhead. There he forced the horses down and tied their muzzles close to the ground, looping the reins through some gnarled roots that he found by kicking with the toes of his boots against the floor of the recess.

The horses down and the danger of their neighing minimized, Ross took his rifle from the saddle sheath, slipped out of the recess, and moved along the wall of the cañon until he reached a point near its mouth, where a huge shoulder jutted out behind a growth of nondescript brush.

He had no more than edged past the brush to the concealment of the shoulder of rock, when the moon burst through a cleft in the hills and a flood of rich yellow light streamed down into the cañon. He knew that if one kept right on going through the cañon, from west to east, one would presently strike a trail that led to the Rio Grande.

He had hoped that the Indians, discovering he and his party had left the gorge trail, would assume they had ridden the other. He wasn't exactly 'yearnin'' for a fight. But he knew that the Indians had not yet discovered the point at which he and Miss Pendleton and Seaton had left the gorge trail. He knew they were searching, and that they were converging toward that point, for the hooting drew closer and more distinct.

At last, after a wait of fully an hour, he heard a low hoot which seemed to come from the point in the gorge at which he had entered the cañon, and he knew as well as if he could see the spot that an Indian had reached there, found the hoof-tracks, and was signaling to his friends.

That Indian must have been impatient or reckless. For he did not wait for his fellows to join him, but came down the sloping bottom of the cañon alone. Ross could hear the slithering of his moccasined feet, could see his shadow, slender and grotesque, stretching down the cañon floor. A serrated fringe of lancelike points that came first into view on the cañon floor told Ross that the Indian was wearing a war bonnet.

The white man heard the distant beating of hoofs and surmised that the Indians were

31

assembling their horses in the gorge near the cañon mouth. They had heard the signal and were answering it, and not many minutes would elapse before they would follow the first Indian.

Ross moved away from the rock wall and stood in the brush at the cañon's edge. The moonlight did not strike him; and he stood silent and motionless until the Indian reached the clump of brush. Then his left hand flashed out, went over the savage's shoulder and was hooked back, drawing the warrior toward him. Ross's hand was over the Indian's mouth, the sinewy fingers and the thumb buried deep into the cheeks. And at the instant Ross's pressure was greatest, the moonlight flashed on his knife.

The weapon vanished, reappeared, to vanish again. The Indian squirmed, twisted, tore vainly at the leathery muscles that held him motionless while the steel searched his vitals. He grew limp, and still he was held. Not until his chin went forward to his chest and his knees sagged did the grip relax. And then he was dragged back into the brush.

There came no sound from the covert, no movement of any kind. Another Indian appeared at the head of the cañon and sent his shadow past the clump of brush in which Ross stood.

The second Indian moved faster than the first, for he evidently felt that the first had

32

gone safely down and there was no need of caution. When he reached the shrubbery that concealed Ross he halted, peered down the canyon. A hand darted out of the brush; drew him in. There ensued a subdued threshing, a low groan of mortal agony. After that there was a sinister silence.

Then Ross stuck his head out of the shrubbery. At the head of the cañon, fairly outlined in the moonlight, stood two more savages. There had been four altogether, it appeared. From the hooting they had done in the late afternoon along the river, there might have been a dozen of them.

Ross stuck his rifle out through the brush, keeping the muzzle in the shadows so that the moonlight might not strike it. When the weapon crashed, one of the Indians toppled forward and came rolling down the floor of the cañon. The other darted for cover, and Ross drew back and waited until he heard rapid hoof-beats from the gorge.

'That's all, eh?' was his thought. 'Four.'

Three of the four would never do any more hooting in the woods.

He stood for some time in a shadow, carefully scrutinizing the floor and walls of the gorge. There were no more hoots.

Ross grinned with malice. His thoughts were derisive. Hooting! Did they think they were cunning? Or was it that they considered the white man could not discriminate between

33

the real and the artificial? He did not answer these questions. He spoke aloud, vindictively drawling: 'Well, do the rest of your hootin' in the happy huntin' grounds!'

He moved back, down the cañon. He found the horses, released them, and retethered them so that they would have some freedom.

'I reckon you can go to sleep now,' he told them aloud. 'That peace party won't bother you any more.'

Lest he frighten Miss Pendleton by approaching her when he knew she was apprehensive of all sound, he drew the saddles from the horses and stretched himself upon the two blankets on a rock ledge far back from the side of the cañon. He laid his rifle beside him and placed his six-shooter between his legs; for though the fourth Indian had gone, there was no telling how soon he might get reinforcements and come back to finish him.

But he thought there would be no further trouble. He sank into a deep sleep, and when he opened his eyes again morning had come.

He climbed up the slope to the rock overhang. While he stood in front of it, wondering if Miss Pendleton and Seaton were awake, he heard her voice:

'Have they gone?'

'Yep.'

Miss Pendleton stuck her head between the

bushes that sheltered the overhang. Her face was drawn and pale; she had evidently slept little. Right now her nerves were tortured, and he felt a pulse of pity for her.

'I heard shooting,' she said. 'Not long after you left here last night. Was it you?'

'I had to let my rifle off once.'

'And the Indians?'

'Shucks,' he replied. 'I shot one, an' the others pulled out.'

'That must have been when I heard horses running down there in the gorge. Did you kill the one you shot at?'

'He's mighty dead by this time, I expect.'

'And did they—You are not—hurt?'

'Nothin' much has happened,' he explained. 'We won't be bothered again unless there's more of them. But that ain't likely. These were young braves that broke away from the reservation. Some of the pride has been taken out of them, an' they'll sneak back.' He gazed about him.

'Mr. Manners around?' he asked.

Contempt and scorn whitened her cheeks and lips. She repressed her anger, however, and Ross felt she was making progress.

'You seem to delight in using that term when speaking of Mr. Seaton,' she said, her voice steady. 'If you do not like him, why speak of him at all? You must know that you have every advantage of him out here. You are armed; you are accustomed to danger, to

35

discomfort; you are inured to this hard life.

'But suppose you were to visit the East. Don't you think you would appear as ridiculous there as you seem to think Mr. Seaton appears here? And do you imagine you are capable of doing the things that Mr. Seaton does in his daily life? Have you the ability to appear in a court of law? Do you know anything of life outside of this section of the world?'

He stood looking straight at her, his face expressionless. And he did not answer. He was not going to argue with her, and she could perceive that her words had made no impression on him.

'When Mr. Manners an' you are ready we'll be goin' on,' he said. 'We won't have any breakfast, for the reason that there ain't any around. But if we make time we'll get where we're goin' by noon.'

He went down the slope to the horses. Later, she and Seaton joined him. In a strained silence they mounted and rode out of the cañon. Miss Pendleton had refused to ride Ross's horse; she had got up with Seaton.

Halfway up the cañon they came upon the body of an Indian. He was lying face down, his headdress crumpled beside him.

The sunlight glinted upon a splash of color at the edge of some brush that fringed a shoulder of the cañon wall, and Miss Pendleton observed that the patch of color was a moccasin. Beyond the moccasin, in the shade of the brush, was the outline of a naked bronzed leg. She shuddered.

She was aware that Ross had lied to her. She did not want to keep thinking of the moccasined foot, but every time she looked at Ross, riding silently ahead, she was reminded of it. There was an explanation for his reticence, too, she supposed.

He would not unnecessarily worry a woman, but she felt she must know what had happened down there in the darkness of the cañon. Some day she would find courage to ask him; that was of course if after he had delivered her and Seaton to the Circle Dot she should ever see him again.

After they had ridden an hour or so she observed that the gorge was broadening. She was looking far ahead, toward a point where the gorge flattened out and seemed to merge with the floor of a basin, when a faint report reached her ears. After an interval there came another report, followed by a half-dozen more in rapid succession. They sounded like the muffled crashing of Ross's rifle in the cañon during the night.

The sounds came from a point nearly straight ahead, and Miss Pendleton was not surprised when she saw Ross turn in the saddle, look back and motion with great urgency. He did not look back again, but put his horse into a run.

37

Ross was soon out of sight beyond a bend in the sloping wall of the gorge; but here the trail was wide and smooth, and she and Seaton had little trouble following it.

They made good time, too, for the horse under them was refreshed and willing. But they could not catch him. After they swept out upon the floor of the basin they had one flashing glimpse of him, far ahead, his horse running with giant strides. After that they observed no movement of any kind.

'Something is happening out there,' observed Seaton, nodding toward the vast reaches of the silent basin. 'Indians again, I suppose. I don't blame Ross for being so touchy. This country is enough to make a savage out of a man!'

They followed the trail over an undulating section until they reached the timber. For several miles the way ran along the edge of the timber; then it abruptly brought them to the banks of a little river. They crossed at the shallow the trail ran through, and emerged from timber on the other side of the stream. The horse halted and neighed.

Directly in front of Miss Pendleton and Seaton were three men. One of the men was Ross; the others were strangers to her. All were standing. Their horses were grazing at a little distance, the reins trailing over their heads.

Not more than thirty or forty feet beyond

the three men were the charred ruins of a building. Some logs, not yet destroyed, were still smouldering.

Near the ruins of the building was a small corral. Directly in front of the corral gate a small fire was smouldering. Near the fire was the huddled body of a man. Close beside him was something over which a blanket had been thrown or laid.

Here and there were other bodies, Indians. They were arrayed like the one Miss Pendleton had seen in the cañon; their faces were hideously painted. Some horses, saddleless, were standing about, grazing. There were a half-dozen dead Indians, and this time Miss Pendleton did not shudder, for she saw what had been done by the red marauders, and felt they deserved the fate that had befallen them.

She and Seaton rode forward. There had evidently been some sort of conference in progress between Ross and the two other men, but now the three were silent. The strangers stared at Miss Pendleton; Ross gazed downward.

Miss Pendleton got down, leaving Seaton in the saddle. She moved forward until she was close to the men. She stood then, clasping and unclasping her hands, staring from one to the other.

They said nothing.

'Oh!' she exclaimed finally. 'This is

terrible!'

'Yes,' said one man, 'it's mighty terrible. It's worse. It's hell!'

The man's voice startled Miss Pendleton; it was the voice of the man Ross had called 'Fagin' two nights ago, when she had stood beside a building in Deming, listening to him as he talked with Ross.

Fagin was tall and slender. His face was thin, the skin was of a texture of leather. He had black, glowing eyes, a big mouth. His nose was large, drooping.

He wasn't a prepossessing man, and yet Miss Pendleton felt vaguely attracted to him. He was singularly confident, sure of himself; and there was a gleam of recklessness in his eyes, a suggestion of mischief of baffling derision. He was an enigma.

She heard Ross speaking softly. He was telling her that the man was Peter Fagin, and that the other man was Brandt Adams. The other night, when she had overheard Ross talking with Fagin, she had heard Ross mention the name. 'If you an' Brandt Adams figure to stay in this country an' keep healthy, you want to keep a considerable distance away from the Circle Dot range!' Ross had told Fagin.

Now, as the men were being introduced to her, she wondered how these men, hostile toward one another, could meet here and speak so calmly and politely.

Fagin and Adams were not effusive. Haltingly, diffidently, they acknowledged the introduction.

'I hope you'll like this country,' said Fagin.

'You sure got here at a bad time,' remarked Adams. 'The Indians ain't in the habit of doin' this thing regular. You just had to get here when it happened.'

'What did happen?' she asked.

Fagin looked at Ross.

'There was a nester named Porter lived here,' said Fagin. 'Him an' his wife an' their daughter. The daughter was about fourteen. Some time last night or this mornin' they must have snuck up. You can see what's left of Porter's shack. The Indians was after horses, I reckon; or mebbe they was just full of the devil, as usual. They built a fire. Over there is what is left of Porter. They'd done worse to his wife. The daughter we ain't been able to find.'

Miss Pendleton felt she would have fainted had not Ross been watching her. Ross's face was grave, but there was a glint in his eyes which told her he expected her to lose her self-control. She wouldn't—not with him watching her. She became aware that all the limpness had gone out of her, that inwardly she had stiffened to meet this crisis. Although she knew that her face was ghastly white and her lips bloodless, she stood rigid, looking straight at Fagin.

41

'We heard shooting,' she said. 'That was you and Mr. Adams, I suppose. But you weren't able to do anything?'

'We got around too late,' replied Fagin. 'We'd just got to that ridge over there, when we seen what was up. We made a clean job of it, but not soon enough to help Porter an' his wife.'

The men stood, their faces glum, staring downward. Miss Pendleton was oppressed with a sensation of terrible helplessness, of futility. She couldn't think of anything that should be done, and she surmised that the same feeling had overtaken the men.

'I got three,' Ross said. 'There were four, an' one got away. I thought that was all. The four must have been members of this other party. They'd been followin' us all afternoon. From Buckner's Flat. That's where we first noticed them. I reckon I hadn't ought to have been so sure. If I'd have come on, maybe I'd have got here in time to help Porter.'

'You're doin' a lot of thinkin' wrong lately,' said Fagin.

Fagin did not remove his gaze from Ross's face, although he smiled with one corner of his mouth at Brandt Adams, who grinned mirthlessly.

'Well,' said Ross, 'any thinkin' that I'm doin' is my own.'

'That's the point,' said Fagin. 'You are all right as long as your thinkin' don't get out

42

where folks can hear it.'

Ross did not answer; although Miss Pendleton knew that here was being carried on more of that conversation she had overheard that night in Deming when she had been standing near the building listening.

Ross raised his head, looked straight at Fagin.

'I reckon we ought to be lookin' for Porter's daughter,' he said.

His words brought the conversation abruptly from the verge of violence to consideration of the unfortunate Porters.

'Yes,' said Adams; 'I reckon we're forgettin'. But it's likely they done for her before we got here.'

Fagin swung on his heel and moved northward, toward some timber. Adams went away westward, toward a bridge. Ross walked toward a shed that still was standing.

Miss Pendleton gazed about, seeking Seaton, who had disappeared while she and the others had been talking. But now she saw him coming out of some brush near the river, southward; and he was leading a little girl.

The girl was small and delicate. She was crying; one hand was covering her eyes as she came forward with Seaton. She was weak from witnessing the massacre and destruction, for her knees gave way and she sank to the ground.

Seaton picked her up in his arms and

carried her. He placed her in a grass clump near where Miss Pendleton had stopped, and the girl sank down and covered her face with her hands.

Fagin, Adams, and Ross came back. They stood helplessly looking down at the girl until Miss Pendleton knelt beside her. Then Ross stuck his hands deep into his pockets and vindictively kicked at a hummock of earth. Fagin and Adams frowned.

For some minutes there was no sound except the half-stifled sobs that came from the writhing figure that Miss Pendleton was kneeling beside. Then Ross and the other men walked away, leaving Miss Pendleton alone with the girl.

Over at the edge of the timber north of the ruins of the house the men mercifully disposed of the bodies of Porter and his wife. When that task had been accomplished they came back to where Miss Pendleton sat in the grass, the girl's head resting in her lap. They stood, sullen and subdued, their animosities dulled by the grief of the Porter girl.

Later they made a meal of the provisions they found in the Porter chuckwagon, which, evidently, the Indians had not taken the pains to search. By the time the meal was finished the afternoon sun was hovering over the peaks of a distant mountain range.

The girl had been quieted. She now sat mute and dazed, staring at the ruins of the house. Ross, Seaton, Fagin, and Adams stood at a little distance from her and Miss Pendleton.

'Well,' said Fagin, 'I reckon we're through here. Nothin' more to be done. We'll be gettin' along.'

He looked at Miss Pendleton, at Ross. He winked at Adams. He spoke to Miss Pendleton.

'When you think she's able to travel, we'll be goin',' he said.

Miss Pendleton stiffened. Her voice was cold and amazed.

'Do you mean that you intend taking her with you?' she asked.

'I reckon,' Fagin replied.

'She ain't got nobody now,' said Adams. 'We'd give her a mighty good home.'

There was a short silence, a tension.

Then Ross spoke. His voice was low, drawling, slightly mocking.

'Shucks,' he said. 'An' you ain't even askin' the girl!'

'Nor you,' sneered Fagin. 'We aim to run our end of this without any advice. You ain't got nothin' to say—understand? We run her a free hand. The kid ain't got no folks. We cut in here in time to keep them Apaches from gettin' her. She belongs to us, an' we're goin' to take her!'

Fagin's voice had a ring of rage in it—rage and malice. Adams stood, bending a little

45

forward from the hips, his muscles tensed.

And now Miss Pendleton perceived that the tragedy which all along had hovered close to Ross and Adams and Fagin was about to break. She read dire purpose in the eyes and manner of Fagin and Adams; a glance at Ross told her that he would not permit the girl to go with the men.

She had a conviction that Fagin and Adams did not really want the girl to go with them; they were merely putting forth that claim as a pretext to finish their trouble with Ross. She got up and moved away a little distance, for she was dismayed over the impending clash. She stood watching and listening.

Ross also seemed to divine what was impending. And yet he betrayed no sign of emotion. He was facing Fagin and Adams; he appeared to be slouching a little; his shoulders had a queer droop. As from the instant she had first seen him, he appeared to Miss Pendleton to be calm, unperturbed, indifferent.

'Fagin,' he said slowly, 'this ain't a question of what you an' Adams want, or what I want. The girl is goin' to do what she wants to do.

'Young lady,' he went on, turning to the girl, 'you take a good long look at me. Then you look just as long as the other men here, an' at this woman. You are goin' with the one looks best to you.'

The girl gazed at Ross; at Fagin, Adams, and Seaton. Her eyes were clouded until she looked at Miss Pendleton. Then she smiled, got to her feet and walked toward that new friend, who held out her hands.

Holding the girl tightly, Miss Pendleton stared at Ross. A change had come over him. The change was not so much in his appearance as in his manner. Until now he had been indifferent, quiet, seemingly ready to yield or to argue.

He now stood rigid, his feet placed a little apart, his legs bending slightly at the knees. His left hand was hanging stiffly at his side, the right hand was rigid, crooked a trifle at the wrist, and drawn up, so that it seemed to hover above the holster of the pistol at his right hip. The fingers of the right hand were spread.

'Right now is the time you've been waitin' for, Fagin!' he said sharply.

The man stood, staring at Ross. At the latter's words Miss Pendleton saw Fagin's eyes fleck with passion; observed the flecks coalesce, noted how the cords of his neck distended. And then, as she still stood watching the man, she saw the intense light die out of his eyes; observed them waver as his gaze drooped.

He had chosen to ignore the challenge.

A flush dyed his cheeks. He folded his arms over his chest and smiled.

'We don't want her that bad, I reckon,' he said.

He turned while Ross silently watched him, walked to his horse and mounted. Adams followed him. The latter's cheeks were aflame.

Once in the saddle, Fagin's manner changed. He smiled derisively, swept his hat from his head and bowed mockingly.

'We'll be seein' you folks again!' he announced.

Fagin and Adams rode northward, their horses in a gallop. When they had faded into the northern horizon, Seaton spoke.

'That's calling their bluff!' he exulted. 'That was a straight-from-the-shoulder way of giving them their choice! Ross, I want to congratulate you! You are the coolest man I ever saw!'

Ross turned. His gaze was level and steady.

'You talk too much, Seaton,' he said.

From that instant until late that night when they reached the Circle Dot ranch, there was little conversation among the four.

It was dark when they rode up beside a big gate. Ross dismounted and spoke shortly:

'This is the Circle Dot. Go right into the house.'

Miss Pendleton and Seaton dismounted and walked away in the darkness toward a rectangle of light that glimmered weakly into the flat desert night. When they neared the lighted doorway she heard Ross's voice as he called to someone named 'Gadd.' She thought at first that he was swearing, and it was not until later that she discovered that he had mentioned a man's name. She heard Ross speaking to someone; his voice was high, sharp, with an edge of command in it.

An atmosphere of emptiness assailed Miss Pendleton. She was aware of thinking that if Mr. Robert M. Nevins lived in this house alone he must be a morose individual.

And now as she waited for someone to answer her call, she resumed wondering about Mr. Nevins. For since she had discovered that she was part owner of a ranch in southern New Mexico, and that she was expected to take an active part in its management, or sell her share to her partner—so the partner had written—she had wondered much about Mr. Nevins.

She had wondered about Mr. Nevins appearance. Was he fat and ugly or slim and good-looking? She felt that her success would depend upon the sort of feeling she would have toward her partner. Would he be what she feared?

She thought not. For if one could judge a man's character from a letter he had written, Mr. Nevins must be a strained, polite, and educated man. For his penmanship had been almost perfection, his diction dignified, his grammar better than her own.

49

'I shall meet you at the Deming station with the buckboard on the sixteenth of April,' he had written; 'and I sincerely hope that our relations may be as pleasant as they should be.'

She was conscious of a thrill of anticipation when she heard a step inside the house. And then she stood smiling, although a little bewildered, when in a farther door appeared a girl of about twenty.

The girl was very good-looking, Miss Pendleton decided. She had a wavy mass of golden-brown hair; the skin of her face and her arms—bared to the elbow—was a rich tan with the satiny bloom of a ripe peach beneath.

'Oh!' she exclaimed, delight in her voice; 'this is Miss Pendleton, isn't it?'

Miss Pendleton's answering smile lacked cordiality.

'Yes,' she said. 'I am Miss Pendleton. Will you kindly tell Mr. Nevins we are here?'

The girl's eyes became perplexed; she took a step forward.

'Why,' she said, 'I thought Bob—Mr. Nevins—was to meet you! I was certain I heard him talking when you rode in!'

Miss Pendleton caught a light that danced in her eyes as she looked beyond the visitor. The Eastern girl turned to see Ross standing behind her in the light from the doorway.

'Bob Nevins,' said the girl; 'what on earth

have you been up to now?'

Miss Pendleton gasped.

'You!' she exclaimed. 'You are Mr. Nevins?'

'I reckon,' he replied. He was amused at her bewilderment. And there was a glint in his eyes which might have been derision. 'Welcome to the Circle Dot, Miss Pendleton,' he said.

## CHAPTER FIVE

Miss Pendleton stared at Nevins, the man she had known as 'Ross'. So far as she could determine, there wasn't anything that looked remotely like emotion in his eyes. She looked for amusement; she had expected it. What she saw was the unconcern and the indifference that had marked his manner toward her since her first meeting with him in Deming.

He had fooled her. She didn't know why. Doubtless he had his reasons, and they must have seemed sufficient to him, for he betrayed no sign of embarrassment or regret. But while she looked at him he spoke.

'A natural mistake, I reckon,' he remarked. 'The "Ross" is a nickname. The boys around here hung it on me when they found I was from Rosswell.'

Miss Pendleton stood rigid, meeting his gaze.

'You came to Deming purposely to meet us, Mr. Nevins?' she said. 'At least you advised us to that effect in your letter.'

'That was what I was there for.'

'And yet you stood there on the station platform and watched us go to the hotel without attempting to reveal your identify?'

'I was there, sure enough.'

'And I presume you had your reasons for not making yourself known?'

'I reckon I had.'

He did not advance his reasons; he made no apology.

Indignation and disdain were two emotions that fought within her for expression. Both were in her eyes as she watched him.

'I suppose you realize that if Mr. Seaton and I had known you were Mr. Nevins we wouldn't have been so—so—'

'Impolite,' he finished.

She bit her lip, withholding speech.

'No,' he went on, betraying a frank interest in her flaming cheeks, 'I suppose you wouldn't have been. But what difference does it make? Ross was the same man as Mr. Nevins. Namin' him don't change him any. Ross wasn't hurt any, an' Mr. Nevins ain't worryin' himself.'

He stepped close to the Porter girl and laid a hand on her head.

'Seems I've heard your name,' he remarked. 'It's Nellie, ain't it?'

The girl nodded.

'Well, Nellie,' he said, 'you run right over there to Grace Rignal.' He pointed to the young woman who had greeted Miss Pendleton. Grace smiled and held out her hands. Nevins watched the young woman lead the child through a doorway. Then he stepped past Miss Pendleton and Seaton and stood smiling.

'Come in,' he said. 'It's likely you'll find this a little crude after what you've been accustomed to. But it's the best we've got, an' you're welcome to it.'

Miss Pendleton wasn't certain that she and Seaton were welcome. Nevins's voice had no cordial ring in it, no enthusiasm. And after his treatment of them, it seemed that he must now be grudgingly offering his hospitality.

Miss Pendleton's hostility had changed into what she felt was a violent hatred and contempt. And yet she could not forget that she was at the Circle Dot as his guest, and that she could not demand more than he chose to give her until her status as part owner had been definitely established. She couldn't offend him in his own house, and yet she had no intention of letting him off without reproof after the way he had treated her.

She stood looking straight at him.

'You wrote that you would meet us with a buckboard,' she said. 'I observed that the buckboard was not in Deming.'

'The buckboard was there.'

'Oh! Then I suppose something must have happened to it?'

'Nothin' happened to it.'

She waited for further explanation. None came.

'Was there anything wrong with the horses belonging to the buckboard?' she questioned.

'You an' Mr. Manners rode them home,' he said.

'Oh! Then perhaps the reason you didn't bring us home in the buckboard was that you were afraid of the Indians?'

He looked intently at her, his eyes gleaming.

'I reckon it wasn't Indians,' he said. And now he almost smiled.

'Gibson could have told you,' he said. 'Why don't you ask him?'

'Gibson?'

'The man who runs the hotel.'

Her gaze was cold, direct.

'I suspected Gibson,' she said. 'I caught him watching us, and I felt he knew more than he admitted. Do you mean to say that Gibson knew that you were deliberately concealing your identity from us?'

'Gibson has known me for a good many years,' he replied. 'Yes, it seems he was

54

concealin' somethin'.'

'That means you didn't care whether we came to the Circle Dot or not!'

'I reckon that's what it means,' he admitted.

Miss Pendleton had expected denial or equivocation. The frank admission startled her, amazed her, gave her a queer, sinking sensation. She knew quite well that at home she had been in the habit of receiving people she did not like. In her circle, for the sake of politeness, there must necessarily be some hypocrisy. Such frankness dismayed her.

'Well!' she exclaimed, stiffening. 'I am glad I learned that! I assure you we shan't bother you any more! We shall ride right back to Deming.'

'I'll have Ben Gadd hook up your horses,' he said.

He moved toward the open doorway, and Miss Pendleton became rigid with indignation and defiance.

'Don't trouble yourself!' she said. 'I believe we have a right to be here! If you will be so good as to show us to our rooms, we shall be glad to take up with you tomorrow my legal claim to my partnership.'

'Sure,' he agreed. He stood in the doorway, his gaze smoothly imperturbable. 'If you'll just sit down an' wait until Grace gets through puttin' Nellie Porter to bed she'll take care of you an' Mr. Manners.'

He turned and stepped out of the doorway into the darkness.

★ ★ ★

Edna Pendleton assured herself that had Nevins not left the house so abruptly she would have carried out her threat to leave the Circle Dot. Never in her life had she hated any man as she hated Nevins; and she felt he must have seen the searing contempt in her eyes when he had said to her: 'If you'll just sit down an' wait until Grace gets through puttin' Nellie Porter to bed she'll take care of you an' Mr. Manners.'

Nevins's persistent use of the term 'Mr. Manners' was positively disgusting. She had expected Nevins to be a gentleman; she found he was a boor: an overbearing, self-sufficient egotist.

But now that she was at the Circle Dot, she was determined to stay. She would demand her rights; she would fight for whatever belonged to her, for she strongly suspected that Nevins had adopted his boorish attitude in order to discourage her from staying.

She and Seaton had not long to wait until Grace Rignal appeared, smiling. She looked at Edna.

'I suppose you are tired,' she said. 'Will you please come with me?'

Edna's lips were stiff and white with the

cold passion that was seething through her, and the gentle warmth in Grace Rignal's eyes barely won a responsive smile from her. She said good night to Seaton, and followed the Rignal girl through a doorway and up some stairs. There was a bracket lamp on the wall in the upper hallway, and in its feeble glare Grace Rignal halted and moved close to Edna.

'He hurt you, didn't he?' she said. A smile, big and winsome, wreathed her lips. 'But you mustn't mind,' she added; 'that's just his way. Something has disturbed him. When you get to know him better you will find him very kind and considerate.'

The something which had disturbed him, Edna knew, was herself. For some reason he had taken a dislike to her, and was taking the most direct way of showing it.

But she was curious about Grace Rignal, and she was amazed to discover that, although the young woman seemed to be warmly sympathetic toward her, she resented the young woman's presence at the Circle Dot. Grace Rignal appeared to have some authority here.

What was her position? Why was she staying at the ranch house with Nevins? Was she a relative, a servant, or a friend?

'You are wondering about me, aren't you?' asked the girl.

Edna flushed. She had been wondering, and she was amazed that the girl had been able to read her thoughts. But when she turned and glanced into the Western girl's clear, keen eyes, she received a distinct shock. She had meant to disclaim any interest in Grace Rignal, but a long, searching look warned her that deceit or equivocation would be futile.

'Naturally, my dear,' she answered.

'I'm glad you didn't deny it,' said Grace. 'I am staying here because I haven't any other place to stay. I am twenty now. When I was fourteen my parents died. We lived about twenty miles west of here, on Dry River. There were no relatives. After Dad and Mother died Bob Nevins brought me here. He treats me like a daughter.'

She stood looking straight into Edna's eyes. Her own gaze was direct and proud. Suddenly the visitor went to Grace and put her arms about the girl.

'We are going to be great friends,' said Edna.

The girl held her tightly for a moment, then went to the door, where she stood smiling.

'You'll like Bob Newman too,' she said. 'You can't help it. He isn't what you think he is!'

After Edna heard Grace's retreating footsteps she stood for several minutes staring at herself in the glass of the dresser. Her lips were tightly pressed together; her eyes held an aggressive light. She felt aggressive. She meant to show Nevins a thing or two before she got through with him. Never in her life had she been so determined.

## CHAPTER SIX

Grace Rignal spent more time upstairs with Edna Pendleton than she had meant to, for she had in mind the fact that the man who had accompanied her to the Circle Dot appeared very tired and sleepy. After leaving the visitor, Grace hurried downstairs.

But Seaton had vanished. Grace stood staring at the chair in which he sat when she left him. The leather bags he had lugged in were on the floor near this chair; and Seaton's hat was on the floor beside them.

The girl went to the outside door, gazed out into the darkness, and then walked to a far corner of the room and dropped into a chair. Seaton, she felt, had not gone far.

To Grace, Seaton was a marvelous person. She had read of people in the East; Nevins had talked to her about them; she had heard them referred to in unflattering terms by various men of the Circle Dot outfit. All her life she had been accustomed to seeing men attired in boots, overalls, woolen shirts, broad-brimmed hats. Most of them had worn chaps, cartridge-belts, pistols, spurs.

Yet to her they held no romance. They were everyday figures, not to be invested with the lure of the new or the unusual. When Seaton had stepped into the doorway of the big room he was not the ridiculous figure he had appeared some hours after leaving Deming. Before leaving the vicinity of the Porter place he had donned a clean shirt, collar, and tie.

He had brushed from his trousers and shoes the dust of travel; he had washed in the stream that ran past the ruins of the Porter cabin. And when he had stepped into the big room of the Circle Dot ranch house to confront Grace Rignal, he was almost as immaculate as when he had stepped from the train at Deming.

Seaton, she had observed, was not so tall as Nevins, nor was he as lithe and slender. In fact, Seaton was rather plump and rounded, though he gave the impression that the surplus flesh concealed good muscles.

Grace did not wait long. When she heard a step outside the doorway a tinge of color surged into her cheeks, and as Seaton entered the room she smiled shyly at him.

'I didn't mean to keep you waiting,' he apologized. 'I—I rather thought you'd be with Miss Pendleton for quite a while; and—and I took a plunge in the creek.'

The girl looked at his damp hair; observed

the new freshness of the skin of his face.

'Everybody seems to have gone,' he said. His voice was uncomplaining; it even expressed mild amusement. 'But I guess we'll get along. I'm Hale Seaton.'

'I am Grace Rignal,' said the girl. 'I told Miss Pendleton you would carry her bags upstairs. Will you?'

Seaton smiled, and the girl blushed again. Once more, in the hall upstairs, after Miss Pendleton's bags had been placed where Grace Rignal directed, the girl blushed. She pointed to a door.

'Your room is there,' she said. And before Seaton could thank her she had vanished down the stairway, and Seaton stood alone in the hallway, his own luggage at his feet.

Once in the room, he sank into a chair near a window and sat for some minutes gazing abstractedly outside. He was tired from the two-day ride and the unaccustomed out-of-doors exercise in which he had been forced to indulge, and he stretched out in the chair in luxurious enjoyment of the cool breeze that swept in at the window. An hour later, beginning to drowse, he got up, undressed, and went to bed.

He had no knowledge of when he went to sleep, but he awakened with a start, aware that he was fighting for breath. Something soft was drawn tightly over his mouth. He was lying flat on his back, and his first thought was that in some manner the blanket which he had pulled over him after he had gone to bed had become twisted and drawn tight over his lips.

He tried to lift a hand to remove the blanket, and was amazed to discover that his hands were tightly bound together, and that both were apparently lashed to the side of the bed.

He twisted his head in an attempt to escape the cumbering cloth that covered his mouth, and when he had got the blanket off his shoulders he discovered that the object which covered his mouth was not the blanket at all. It was more like a handkerchief.

He could think of no reason why anyone should play such a trick on him.

Nevins wouldn't. He was sure of that. Nevins was too serious-minded to play tricks. He was a bit sullen, perhaps, but there was an undoubted dignity in his sullenness which would make the perpetration of such a practical joke impossible.

It was ridiculous to suppose that Grace Rignal would do such a thing, or that Miss Pendleton would even consider it. As a matter of fact, Seaton's thoughts did not dwell upon either of the young women more than a fraction of a second. With Nevins eliminated, there remained only the cowboys at the ranch to be considered.

Seaton considered them. He decided that it

was very likely they would play a practical joke on him, although when he had taken his plunge in the creek he had passed close to a low, squat building which might have been the quarters of the men who worked on the place, and its windows had been dark. They hardly would attempt a joke on him until they at least had seen him. But here he was, helpless.

He found he wasn't very apprehensive. He had no enemies in this section of the country; he could think of no reason why any one should attempt to harm him. He was more impatient than frightened, although he felt that until he discovered the intentions of whoever was in the room with him he had better offer no resistance.

Listening, he heard no sound. Lying motionless, his senses beginning to strain in spite of his effort to be patient, he felt the bed tremble slightly. Simultaneous with the vibration of the bed he heard a low grunt, such as sometimes accompanies great physical effort. Then, having reached the end of his patience, he raised his head, twisted his body, and peered over the side of the bed as a dark form arose from the floor.

He could see the dim outlines of a man's figure bending over him. And before he could move again, a big hand was pressed against him and his head was forcibly jammed back upon the pillow.

There was an apparent fury in the pressure of the man's hand. At least, there was sufficient force to convince Seaton that he was not the victim of a joke, and that whoever was in the room had a sinister object in view.

Only his feet and legs were free, and he drew his knees up in an effort to get leverage to twist his body away from the intruder. But before he could begin the movement, the man sat heavily upon his legs, pinning him down. And then, quite calmly it seemed to Seaton, the man seized his bound hands, pressed them tightly against his chest, and slipped a rope over his head.

The rope had a noose in it. It tightened so that Seaton could feel the knot against his neck just below the ear. Desperate now, he made a gigantic effort to escape the man's grip. He failed. The noose around his neck tightened, shutting off his breath. The noose was held there, steadily, firmly, viciously, despite Seaton's terrible threshing and squirming.

The unknown man was intent on murder. He was coldly and deliberately sitting there, steadily tightening the noose.

Seaton's senses were going, but he could make no outcry for help. Twinkling points of light began to dance in his vision; pinwheels of fire flamed before his eyes; the world became a swirling chaos of leaping, dancing sparks set in blackness.

He thought he was being lifted and carried. Finally there came a sensation of falling, slowly, gently, into an abysmal silence.


## CHAPTER SEVEN

'I'm cussed if he didn't try to hang himself!'

The exclamation came from a tiny voice at a great distance. The voice was high, querulous, amazed. Others followed it.

'I reckon he don't like himself a heap,' said one.

'He'd been a goner in a minute more,' said another. 'Me an' Slim was moseyin' around, not bein' able to sleep. We'd got a drink at the windmill an' was comin' around the corner of the bunkhouse when I seen somethin' swingin' back an' forth alongside the house, under the dude's winder. We busted right over. An' gentlemen, don't whisper! There was the dude, hangin' by his neck with his tongue out! 'Course we cut him down, an' he slumped like a bag of wet meal. Mighty narrow squeak!'

There were other voices. A woman's scream. Miss Pendleton's Seaton had no difficulty in recognizing it. Grace Rignal's voice. Soft hands on his forehead; on his neck, which seemed to have been seared with a red-hot iron.

When he at last opened his eyes he looked straight into those of Grace Rignal, who was bending over him as he lay on the ground, bathing his face and throat with water.

He tried to tell her that he was all right now, but no sound came from his lips, and so he smiled in an attempt to reassure her. But he wondered who had got the impression that he had tried to hang himself. Evidently whoever had said that had not seen that his hands were tied together and that it would have been impossible for him to have hanged himself.

Grace's eyes were filled with grave reproach. Did she, too, think he had tried to commit suicide? It seemed she did. All of them thought so, for they stood around him, a dozen or so men and the two girls, mingled commiseration and derision in their glances.

'Figured to do a good job,' said a man who stood at a little distance. Seaton could not see his face. 'Tied the rope to the bedpost an' jumped out of the window. Curious he didn't break his fool neck, first pop!'

Seaton was aware of a sudden rage that surged through him. These men were callous; they could stand around and make crude jokes over what might easily have been a tragedy; but they could not use their brains in an effort to get at the truth. They were too ready to believe the worst about anyone. And while they senselessly jabbered, the would-be

66

murderer was making his escape.

The blood was rushing back into Seaton's brain. He was thinking more clearly now, and his resentment against the men was growing. And when he heard one of them ask where 'the dude' had got the rope, another picked up the noose which had been around Seaton's neck and closely examined it.

'Why, hell!' exclaimed the man in a hoarse whisper, 'this here is Bob Nevins's rope! Now where in hell did he get it? Last I seen of it, it was hangin' on that old saddle of Bob's, in the lean-to!'

'Hell! look here!' exclaimed another man. He was standing near, examining several short pieces of rope which he had picked up a little distance from the house. He was puzzled; he looked at the ropes and then at Seaton.

'Mebbe the packin' ain't all out of this case yet!' he said; 'these ropes has been knotted an' cut!' He stood erect, his eyes glowing as though he had been seized by an inspiration; then he suddenly dived forward to where Seaton sat.

'Lemme see your wrists!' he demanded. And before Seaton could resist he had grabbed the wrists and was inspecting them. Seaton's flesh still showed where the rope had sunk in. The skin was bruised; a black-and-blue line ran almost around the wrists.

The cowboy stood up again.

'That's it, eh?' he exclaimed. 'These here ropes has been round the dude's wrists! They was cut after he'd been swung!' He looked down at Seaton, and his voice was authoritative. 'Mr. Man,' he said, 'I reckon it's up to you to tell just what happened!'

But Seaton had no intention of informing them of what had occurred. He was still enraged over the thought that the men had been so quick to accuse him of the crime of attempted self-destruction. He looked at Grace Rignal and spoke as coldly as his stiffened tongue and lips would permit.

'Please tell them that what happened to me is none of their business,' he said.

The man who had discovered the short rope stiffened, and smiled derisively.

'On the prod, eh?' he said shortly. 'A heap insulted. Well, bed suits me, an' I ain't never goin' to be interested in dudes again!'

There were smiles, short dry laughs. The men began to move away toward the bunkhouse.

Seaton got to his feet and stood there swaying slightly from weakness. And he saw Miss Pendleton standing near, very erect, pale.

She called sharply to the man who had found the rope which had bound Seaton's wrists.

'Please send Mr. Nevins here!' she said. 'I

68

want him to explain how a guest in his house happened to be almost murdered with Mr. Nevins's own rope!'

There was a dead silence. Then a voice, not that of the man who had found the rope, answered reluctantly.

'Nevins ain't here,' he said. 'His hoss is gone, an' his saddle!'

★　　★　　★

When Nevins told Miss Pendleton, answering her threat to leave the Circle Dot, that he would have Ben Gadd hook up the horses for her and Seaton, so that, if they desired, they might return to Deming, he hadn't been pretending indifference.

When he first glanced at Miss Pendleton as she stepped from the train at Deming he felt keen disappointment in her. It was founded upon his instant comprehension of her character. He had not made himself known to her at once because he wanted to corroborate his first impression. Later, an impulse of obstinacy or antagonism kept him silent.

She wasn't the type of girl he expected her to be. He had some expectation, aroused from his knowledge of her father, that she would be straightforward, frank, and impulsive, with a personality which would make him eager to do things for her.

She proved to be the reverse type. She was

self-sufficient, intolerant, complaining, arrogant. With her first glance at him he perceived in her what seemed to him to be contemptuous insolence. And at that instant he lost interest in her.

To be sure, he intended to accord her full dues; and he had decided he would not quarrel with her. Also, he meant to reveal his identity sooner. But he hadn't. His antagonism toward her had grown. He wasn't likely to let that antagonism show, because as his guest and partner she was entitled to certain privileges and services, but he had decided that he would make no special effort to entertain her. He'd let Seaton do the entertaining.

His feelings toward Seaton were negative. He didn't dislike the man, nor did he like him. Seaton impressed him as being of negligible importance. He couldn't even become angry at Seaton.

Nevins hadn't unsaddled his horse when he had arrived at the Circle Dot ranch house with Seaton, Miss Pendleton, and the Porter girl; and when he emerged from the house after telling his guests that Grace Rignal would look after their comfort, he walked to the corral gates, mounted, and rode westward.

Watt Hamlin, he knew, was worried about his wife. He had been worried since she left him. She hadn't told him that she found another man whom she liked better than Hamlin. Hamlin declared he would not search for his wife; he pretended to be indifferent. Yet Nevins, knowing Hamlin rather well, because the man had worked for him for several years, had become convinced that Hamlin was brooding over his wife's infidelity. And on the day before that on which Nevins left the Circle Dot to ride to Deming to meet Miss Pendleton he had purposely ridden past Hamlin's cabin, which was snuggled among some timber near the bank of Dry River, about ten miles west of the Circle Dot.

He had found Hamlin sitting on the threshold of the front door, staring dejectedly into distance. The man had not heard Nevins riding up, which proved that he was again in a fit of abstraction.

'Work an' you are gettin' to be strangers,' suggested Nevins. He did not dismount, but sat crossways in the saddle, smiling at Hamlin.

Hamlin was a tall man, and slender. Formerly he had been active, clear-eyed, cheerful. He now smiled mirthlessly. His eyes held an expression of intense dejection.

'I'm sort of slowin' up, I reckon, Bob,' he admitted.

Hamlin was not likely to complain. He did not refer to his wife during the conversation that ensued. It was Nevins who broached the

71

subject, obliquely, gently, when he got ready to leave.

'I'm figurin' on ridin' to Deming tomorrow,' he said. 'Would you be interested in hearin' about anything that's happened?'

Hamlin raised his head and looked straight at Nevins.

'There ain't no use beatin' about the bush, Bob,' he said. 'I always was a heap interested in her. I don't seem to get over it. If you can get word to her, tell her that if she should happen to get around this way again I ain't holdin' nothin' ag'in' her.'

Nevins saw her in Deming. And now, in order to relieve Hamlin's mind, he had taken the first opportunity to ride to the latter's cabin to tell him of his conversation with the recreant wife. He had good news for Hamlin. The woman was coming back just as soon as she could contrive to leave the Tucson man, whose name, Nevins had learned through Gibson, was Matt Blandell.

Nevins crossed the river, observing with a smile that there was a light inside the cabin. That meant, of course, that Hamlin had not yet gone to bed.

Nevins dismounted at the gate of a small corral, hitched his horse to one of the top rails, and walked toward the cabin. The light was in the kitchen; the front room was dark.

Nevins halted at the kitchen door, which was wide open. He peered inside and saw no

72

one. But his quick glance showed him that the kitchen was spotlessly clean; and for a moment, while he stood in the doorway, he wondered at Hamlin's neatness and diligence. It was as if a woman had been at work in the kitchen.

He called. Receiving no answer, he entered the kitchen, crossed it, and halted in the doorway leading from the kitchen into the other room. He peered into the darkened room and called once more.

He heard a sound from a corner of the room, and by shading his hands from the light in the kitchen he could dimly discern the shape of a bed. The white sheet was visible in the faint light of the moon which entered a nearby window. Upon the bed was a dark form.

Hamlin had lain down fully dressed. That was Nevins's thought. Hamlin had finished his supper, had cleared up the kitchen. Tired, dejected, he had stretched out for a nap.

Standing in the lighted doorway he called again. He expected Hamlin would sit up and look at him. Then he would give his news.

But Hamlin did not stir at the sound of Nevins's voice. He was evidently a heavy sleeper.

Nevins drew a match from a pocket, lit it, and held it above his head, so that he could see the form on the bed, and so that Hamlin, awakened by the light, could see who had disturbed him.

When the flickering beams of light from the match reached the bed, Nevins drew a quick breath. The match fell to the floor as Nevins darted forward.

Leaning over the bed he shook Hamlin, ran his hands over the man's face and chest. His right had struck an obstruction. A knife handle! The knife was buried in Hamlin's left side!

Again he bent over the inert body. All his senses were acute, his muscles rigid and straining.

Hamlin was dead! Nevins had brought his good news too late.

Nevins backed away from the bed. His first thought was that Hamlin had killed himself. The second was a suspicion that the man had been murdered.

Nevins stood in the subdued light, listening. Hamlin's body was not yet cold, and there was a chance that the murderer was still lurking around.

Nevins moved to the front door, opened it, and cautiously looked out. The moon was shining down into the clearing that surrounded the cabin, and Nevins could hear no sound, detect no movement.

He closed the door and moved toward the kitchen. Halfway across the room a sound reached his ears, and he stood, his gun instantly drawn, his gaze upon the outside

74

door of the kitchen, through which, it seemed to him, the sound had come.

His first thought was that the murderer was coming back to make sure he had completed his work. But instead of the slinking form he expected to see, there came a woman's white hand upon the door-jamb, then the sleeve of a gingham dress, and then the woman herself stood in the doorway, smiling, her eyes eager.

The woman was Hamlin's wife.

## CHAPTER EIGHT

The garment Mrs. Hamlin wore was a house dress. She was without cloak or hat. She had evidently been at the cabin for some time, and Nevins's impression was that she had gone out of the house on some errand, leaving Hamlin to complete his nap. To Nevins her presence explained the condition of the kitchen; while the eager light in her eyes convinced him that she had no knowledge of what had happened to Hamlin.

He stood back a little distance from the door of the darkened room, beyond the flickering light from the lamp in the kitchen, and Mrs. Hamlin did not see him until he walked forward and stood in the doorway. Then for an instant she stood, rigid, her lips parted, staring at him. He saw her gaze directed at his hands, and he looked down, to see that the left, hanging at his side, was stained with Watt Hamlin's blood.

Then as though in a frenzy of apprehension, she leaped past Nevins and ran to the bed. From her lips issued scream upon scream: a ringing, plaintive wail that split the silence with a terrible resonance.

His senses for the moment were all definitely centered upon her. He was not aware of a sound that came from the outside kitchen door; he did not hear steps upon the kitchen floor; and it was not until a form appeared in the doorway leading from the darkened room to the kitchen that he realized that someone had entered and was standing near. Then he wheeled swiftly, to see Brandt Adams and Peter Fagin close to him.

Both Adams and Fagin had drawn their guns. Fagin, standing in front of Adams, was holding his tight against his side, the muzzle leveled at Nevins. Behind Fagin showed Adams's evil visage; his gun was shoved past Fagin's shoulder. Its muzzle, too, was menacing Nevins.

'What's wrong here?' demanded Fagin. 'We heard Mrs. Hamlin screamin'!' A snarl bared his teeth when he observed the gun in Nevins's hand.

'Drop that gun or I'll bore you!' he commanded.

Nevins did not change position or

expression. His face, in the light from the kitchen lamp, was grey with sympathy for Mrs. Hamlin, but in his eyes burned contempt for the two men who had so abruptly appeared.

'When did you think you could order me to do anything, Fagin?' he said steadily. He met the other's eyes, and the flaming flecks in his own revealed his passionate hatred, coldly repressed.

'You're as big a fool as ever, Fagin,' he went on, his voice seeming to lash the other. 'Always rearin' up on your hind legs lookin' for trouble. Always tryin' to turn your wolf loose. Some day I'll get tired of you pokin' your gun around that way. An' then you'll wish you hadn't been so punctual.'

He deliberately walked away from the two men and stooped over Mrs. Hamlin.

'He was dead when I came in,' he said gently. 'I had come over here to tell him what you said: that you'd come back. It was dark in here—just like it is now. I lit a match an' saw him lyin' there. I ran my hands over him an' found the knife.'

'Knife!' she sobbed. 'Oh! oh!'

'I'm a heap sorry,' he said.

The woman had grown quieter, although she still crouched at the side of the bed. She was beating her hands together over Hamlin's body.

Nevins left her and stood before Fagin and

Adams, who had not moved from the doorway.

'You've done a lot of talkin',' he said. 'Where was you when you heard Mrs. Hamlin screamin'?'

'We'd just left her,' answered Fagin. 'We'd been down the creek a-ways, lookin' for some strays. Comin' back we run into Mrs. Hamlin standin' under a tree. "Watchin' the moonlight," she told us. She'd got back to Hamlin this afternoon. She'd started from Deming a day ahead of us. That's how she missed them redskins. She was feelin' pretty happy. She said Hamlin was takin' a nap. While we was talkin' we heard a hoss runnin'. She lit out, thinkin' it was Hamlin goin' somewheres.

'We headed north, toward home. But we'd only gone a little piece when we heard her screamin'.' He moved into the room. 'Hamlin was knifed, you say?'

Adams had walked away from the door; he now returned bearing a lamp, which he had lighted in the kitchen. A thin layer of dust covered the raw bronze of his face and neck; his eyes were glowing and curious as, holding the lamp and pausing in the middle of the room, he stared at Hamlin's body on the bed.

A long look, and then he placed the lamp on a center table and looked at Nevins.

'Plumb center,' he said sententiously.

He walked to the side of the bed, leaned

78

over and peered at the handle of the knife, which was of buckhorn, and soiled with use. After glancing at the knife he stood erect and looked at Fagin.

'Get her out of here!' he said, indicating Mrs. Hamlin.

While Fagin was busy with Mrs. Hamlin, Adams stood, his gaze blank, shifting. But when Fagin reentered the room and closed the door, Adams walked to Hamlin's body and drew out the knife. He stood facing the lamp and examined the handle. It appeared that his examination was largely corroborative, for as he looked at the handle he nodded his head as though in affirmation of a previous conviction.

Abruptly he passed the knife to Fagin, who took it and also examined the handle. His eyes widened and glittered. His lips twitched in an odd smile. He looked at Adams and nodded. He passed the knife to Nevins.

'Take a look,' he suggested.

Nevins had been aware of the pantomimic actions of the two men. They were agreed upon something; something which gave them great satisfaction. The instant he took hold of the knife he knew what that something was. The knife was his; it bore his initials, boldly carved on the handle!

He examined the knife, held it between the thumb and forefinger of his left hand by the tip of the blade, and looked at the two men, one after the other. His gaze was steady and grave. He knew the men were convinced that he had killed Hamlin.

'Looks awkward,' he said.

'Mighty awkward,' affirmed Fagin.

'You was bringin' him good news,' said Adams with broad sarcasm.

Nevins stood watching the two men. They felt no pity for Hamlin or Hamlin's wife; their dominant emotion was a malicious satisfaction over the fact that appearances indicated the guilt of their enemy. Here was an opportunity to dispose of him without risk to themselves. A word to the sheriff, and Nevins would trouble them no more.

The men were not going to try to hold him. He knew that from the way they looked at him. They were not eager for gun play. But Nevins knew that as soon as he left the cabin they would ride to Deming to tell the sheriff what they had discovered.

Fagin laughed.

'Seems there'll be some explainin' to do,' he said.

'Not to you,' Nevins replied.

'Well, I ain't eager to hear the details. Knifin' a man ain't in my line. There ain't nothin' I want to learn about it. But Sheriff Callahan will be mighty interested. He's dead against knife-slingin'. We'll be glad to tell what we know about this deal—'

Too late Fagin threw up a fending arm.

80

Nevins's fist flecked the upraised elbow, smashed against Fagin's jaw, and Fagin went down with a crash that shook the cabin. He squirmed on the floor and tried to draw his gun.

But a boot heel ground his wrist on the board floor, and he screamed in agony as the gun was kicked out of his hand to go thudding against the wall in a corner.

Adams had not moved. He had meditated movement, but his right hand had paused, rigid, six inches from the butt of his gun when he caught the glint of metal at Nevins's side in the confused instant following Fagin's fall. Adams now stood motionless, facing Nevins.

Fagin sat up, his hands on the floor to brace his swaying body. His chin was on his chest; he did not meet Nevins's eyes. Adams could not meet them. He stood staring downward.

'Get up, Fagin!' commanded Nevins.

Nevins stood motionless while Fagin got up and swayed back and forth on unsteady legs. Then Nevins spoke again.

'You boys would like to be bad, I reckon,' he said mockingly. 'But you ain't got the nerve. I'm sick of lookin' at your ugly mugs, an' I'm yearnin' to be alone. Unbuckle your gun belts an' drop them. Then get out of here an' hit the breeze before I turn my wolf loose!'

He watched, his gaze saturnine, while the men obeyed his orders. They walked out at the front door when Nevins opened it for them; and Nevins stepped outside and stood in the shadows beside the cabin as they moved through the moonlight to their horses. A little longer he watched them, until, after crossing a clear sweep of plain, he saw them vanish over the crest of a rise.

Then he reentered the house, closed the front door after him, stood for an instant near the bed, looking down at Hamlin, and opened the door leading to the kitchen.

Mrs. Hamlin was sitting in a chair at the kitchen table, her head resting on her arms, crying.

Nevins walked close and stood looking at her. He laid a hand on her shoulder.

'I reckon you couldn't help hearin',' he said. 'Them boys talked loud enough. It was my knife. Do you think I killed Hamlin?'

She shook her head negatively. She raised her eyes and looked at him.

'Why, it was you who told me he wanted me; that he had forgiven me!' she said. 'It couldn't have been you! You had no reason to kill him. He always liked you.'

He didn't question her about Fagin and Adams, for he knew neither of them could have committed the crime. For the murder had been done with his own knife, which he had lost in the cañon where he had killed the three Indians; and Fagin and Adams could not have found the knife, for they had been far ahead at the time, on the trail toward the Porter cabin. They might have gone back and found the knife, but that was improbable, because there had been so little time.

He sat in the kitchen with Mrs. Hamlin until dawn came. Then he performed his last service for Hamlin. Later, he sat in the saddle near the kitchen door, looking down at Mrs. Hamlin, huddled on the step, her head bowed in her hands.

'I reckon I'll be goin', maa'm,' he said. 'I'm a heap sorry. If there's anything I can do I'd be mighty glad to do it.'

'There is nothing,' she replied. 'But, oh!' she added, 'I wish things had been different!'

## CHAPTER NINE

When Nevins reached the Circle Dot the men of the outfit, except Ben Gadd, were gone.

At the gate of the horse corral Gadd answered Nevins's question.

'They've rode east,' he said, 'to Colter's Flat. With the wagon.'

Gadd was an elderly man. His face was thin, wrinkled. Long, sparse white hair drooped over his ears. He was thinking of the attempted hanging of Hale Seaton. He longed to speak of it. But, perceiving the grimness of Nevins's face, he forbore to question. It had been his experience that 'the boss always knew what he doin'.'

And so Nevins reached the house in ignorance of what had happened.

He found Grace Rignal in the kitchen, preparing breakfast. He greeted her with a smile, and was on the point of telling her about Watt Hamlin when he saw Miss Pendleton standing in the doorway that led from the kitchen to the small rear porch.

Edna had seen Nevins before he had observed her. He had expected she would be rather stiff and formal after his indifference to her the night before, and he expected to find her resentful also. But he was not prepared for the contempt he saw in her eyes, nor the rage that the paleness of her face revealed.

However, as from the first instant he had seen her, her manner aroused in him a malicious antagonism. She had, he had long ago decided, been permitted to have her own way too much. She was accustomed to authority and, not having the proper mental balance, she had become arrogant. It was too bad, too, he felt, for she was a handsome girl and could make herself winsome.

He smiled gravely and asked her if she had slept well after her ride.

She drew herself up; her eyes flashed with cold accusation.

84

'Why don't you ask Hale Seaton that question?' she said coldly.

'I intend to,' he answered quietly, wondering at the mystery of her manner.

'I shouldn't think you would dare to ask him,' she declared, 'after what happened last night!'

His start was inward; he gave no visible sign of emotion. So the Circle Dot had already been informed of the murder of Hamlin. Fagin and Adams were losing no time in spreading the news. And Edna Pendleton had been quick to believe him guilty.

'Well,' he said, 'I'm a heap sorry. My knife too.' He was convinced that Fagin and Adams had mentioned details. They would make the most of their opportunity. He looked gravely at Edna. 'I reckon I'll have to ask you to prove certain things for me before I can get clear of this deal. You remember when we rode out of that cañon, where we holed up to throw the Indians off the trail?'

She nodded. Her eyes were wide, filled with wonder.

'You heard me shoot durin' the night, I reckon?' At her nod he went on: 'I got one Indian with that shot. You saw him lyin' there the next mornin'. You saw somethin' else; I noticed you lookin'. A leg an' a foot stickin' out of the brush beside the cañon.'

'Yes,' she said.

'The leg belonged to one of two Indians I had to knife. Both were in the brush. I lost my knife there.'

'What has that to do with what happened last night?' she asked.

'A heap, I reckon,' he replied. 'Whoever killed Watt Hamlin last night used my knife doin' it.'

'Watt Hamlin is dead?' asked Grace Rignal. She stood at the stove.

'Why, yes,' he answered. 'I thought you had heard about it. Watt was murdered. When I got there last night he was lyin' on the bed in his room with my knife stickin' in him. I'd gone over there to tell Watt that I'd seen his wife in Deming, an' that she said she was comin' back to him. She was already there. She'd started for home before we did.'

He looked at Edna and saw that her eyes were incredulous, disbelieving.

'Yes,' she said coldly; 'I believe I can testify that I heard only one shot in the cañon and that I saw a moccasined foot sticking out of some bushes, but after what you did here last night you could hardly expect any one to believe you!' she asserted scornfully.

'Last night?' he inquired. 'Here? Maybe you'd tell me what happened?'

'Of course you would try to deny it. But I think the evidence is strong enough. It was your rope!'

'What was my rope?' he asked. He looked
86

at Grace. 'Maybe my brain ain't workin' so fast this mornin',' he said. 'Or maybe I'm supposed to know somethin' I don't know. Miss Pendleton seems to be tryin' to tell me somethin'. Maybe you could help her?'

'Some time before midnight some one hanged Mr. Seaton,' Grace told him, filling in the details.

'The boys hear any one around?' asked Nevins.

'No,' answered Grace. 'At first we thought Mr. Seaton had tried to hang himself. But the men found that his hands had been tied.'

Nevins looked at Edna. He walked close to her and held her gaze. He laughed softly, with genuine mirth, his eyes gleaming with amusement. It was as if he was discovering something new in her character.

'You stick by your friends, don't you?' he said. 'An' you ain't afraid to speak right out in meetin'!'

Edna perceived incipient admiration in his eyes, the dawning of respect; the respect a mature man accords a child which under his eyes has developed a new trait of character, commendable, sturdy. But behind that respect was derision, subtle, mocking, which was in his eyes every time he had looked at her.

'An' you think I tried to hang Mr. Manners,' he added. 'That's right charitable of you.'

He turned from Edna to Grace.

'Where is Seaton now?' he asked.

'He went outside a while ago.'

Nevins found Seaton leaning against the fence which spanned the creek, an enclosure in which there were a half-dozen steers.

Seaton's neck bore the burn of the rope that had been around it. But otherwise he appeared to have recovered from his experience. And he grinned broadly when he saw Nevins.

His raiment was as gorgeous as ever, but the petulance he had exhibited during the first days of his acquaintance with Nevins had vanished. His gaze was now steady, grave, direct.

Nevins had expected the man would be in a complaining mood; he was astonished when Seaton greeted him with a grin. His own eyes glinted with the first cordiality the Easterner had seen in them, and Seaton felt a pulse of exultation.

'So you had a narrow squeak, eh?' said Nevins. 'I reckon right now you're feelin' about halfway between prayin' an' cussin'. If you're wantin' to cuss, you can go right ahead. I'll know what's urgin' you.' He looked straight at Seaton. 'Seems there's folks around here that think I had a hand in tryin' to hang you.'

'Don't include me Nevins,' Seaton said. 'I know I've acted like an ass. I know that I insulted you, and that you had a right to treat me as you did. I know you don't like me. But I also know that if you and I ever have any trouble, there won't be any sneaking about it.'

'You didn't get a look at the man?'

'No. I had put out the light. I was asleep. When I awoke I was gagged.'

'You know what time it happened?'

'Around midnight, I think. For the moon was directly overhead, and it came up early.'

About midnight, Nevins stood reflecting. It probably had been about ten-thirty when he discovered Hamlin's body. Hamlin's cabin was about ten miles distant.

'The man who tried to hang you could have been the man who killed Watt Hamlin,' he said. 'He'd have had plenty of time to get here afterward.'

He told Seaton of his experience at the Hamlin cabin. And after he had concluded, Seaton smiled.

'That makes it look bad for you,' he said. 'But of course it's nonsense to think that you would do a thing like that!'

'There's plenty will think it,' Nevins explained.

Abruptly he left Seaton and walked toward the house. He spent some time inspecting the ground under the window from which Seaton had been suspended. He went into the lean-to and examined the saddle from which the rope had been taken.

Then he walked to an outbuilding and spent some time inspecting the ground in the vicinity. He found hoof tracks, where a horse had stood and pawed. But if he discovered any evidence of the identity of the culprit through his examination, he kept his knowledge to himself.

As a matter of fact, there was no further reference to the incident. During the day he sent Grace Rignal over to Hamlin's cabin to visit Mrs. Hamlin. In the girl's absence he summoned Miss Pendleton and Seaton to the room he used as an office, and showed them the articles of partnership which were signed by him and Miss Pendleton's father.

After Seaton and Miss Pendleton read the agreement, Miss Pendleton spoke:

'According to this agreement I have a full half-interest in the Circle Dot—stock, buildings, land, and equipment.'

'That's right.'

Edna looked steadily at him. Her cheeks were a trifle flushed.

'Your letter apprising me of Father's interest in this ranch was the first intimation we had that Father had such an interest. We found no copy of this agreement among his effects.'

'That's likely,' said Nevins. 'Jim was always a little careless.'

'Or he must have trusted you,' Edna

suggested.

'Jim Pendleton was honest himself. He couldn't imagine anybody bein' crooked with him,' he said.

Edna's cheeks blazed. It seemed to her that in Nevins's speech had been a subtle jibe for her own suspicions. And his attitude—the fact that he had written to inform her of her ownership of an interest instead of waiting for her father's heirs to come and claim it—and perhaps take legal steps to force recognition of that interest—was distinctly unusual. Over her stole the conviction that she had been premature in her judgment; the man who sat near her was disclosing an honesty and fairness that startled her.

'Well,' she said, 'I want to thank you for your attitude in this matter. I rather expected to have some difficulty in reaching a settlement. Did Father have a copy of this agreement?'

Nevins reached in his desk and drew out another copy of the agreement, which he held out to her.

'There were two copies. Jim left his here. Scared he would lose it.'

She gave him a quick glance.

'But I presume there is a record of the transaction in the courthouse at Deming?'

'Jim didn't think it necessary to have a record of the deal.'

'Why, then,' she remarked, amazed, 'it

wouldn't have been necessary for you to let us know at all! If you hadn't written to me I should not have known that I had such an interest. You held a clear title. Isn't that so, Hale?'

'Correct,' assented Seaton.

Edna Pendleton felt strangely humbled. Within the last few minutes her opinion of Nevins had changed so rapidly that she was almost breathless with amazement and wonder.

'Well,' she said, no longer arrogant and haughty, 'I—I wish to apologize.'

'For what?' he asked.

'For—for—' She hesitated. 'You understand that I did not know what I should find here,' she went on more steadily. 'I was afraid we might have trouble. That you wouldn't be—that you would be difficult to deal with.'

'I reckon I understand,' he said. 'You thought I'd be crooked. Well, I saw that. It hasn't bothered me.'

He got up and looked down at the copy of the agreement lying on the desk. He tapped it with a forefinger.

'Well,' he said, 'there you are. There's your authority. When do you expect to start?'

'When do I expect to start what?' she asked.

'To run things,' he returned, watching her with a smile which was a little twisted with derision. 'That's what you are expected to do. You've got to learn the business, for I reckon I won't always be here. An' there's a heap of things to learn.' He paused, almost smiled. 'An' a heap of things for a stranger to unlearn,' he added. 'You've made a good beginnin' just now. You've confessed that you've made mistakes. You'll make more. An' if you've got the right stuff in you you'll grow. If you don't grow you'll be no good here. That's straight talk, but you've been needin' it.'

He went out, mounted his horse and rode eastward, while Miss Pendleton and Seaton, in the office, looked at each other.

Both their faces were grave, for they had received a new revelation of Nevins's character, and the revelation had somehow helped them to reappraise themselves.

'Well,' Seaton observed finally, 'I wonder if we have been as important as we thought we were.'

## CHAPTER TEN

Nevins was absent from the ranch house for two days. On the morning of the third day he rode in to the ranch. He talked for a few minutes with Grace Rignal about Mrs. Hamlin.

For the present Mrs. Hamlin meant to remain at the cabin. She had no plans for the future. Grace had stayed with her the entire day. After Nevins left the Hamlin cabin, Fagin had returned. He had taken the knife which had been used to kill Hamlin—Nevins's knife. He had told Mrs. Hamlin he was taking the weapon to Sheriff Callahan at Deming.

He asked Grace about Edna Pendleton and Seaton.

'Miss Pendleton has been riding some,' Grace informed him. 'It seems she's getting acquainted. Mr. Seaton has spent a great deal of time around the house. He says he doesn't care much about riding.'

He spent the morning in his office, getting his desk straightened up. At the noon meal he had very little to say to Seaton or Edna Pendleton, although he civilly answered questions Edna asked about the ranch.

He got away as soon as he could and spent some time in the harness shop. Late in the afternoon he emerged from the shop, looking for Ben Gadd. He wanted to tell Gadd about a particular set of harness.

Standing just outside the door of the harness shop he saw Edna Pendleton, Grace Rignal, and Seaton on the porch. Nellie Porter was sitting on the edge of the porch, sewing. The others were in chairs. Standing on the ground at the edge of the porch,

94

evidently having just dismounted, was a man, a stranger.

Nevins had been expecting a visit from Sheriff Callahan. Callahan was a friend, but Callahan was also an officer of the law, and if Fagin and Adams had gone to him with a report of the killing of Watt Hamlin, Callahan would have to do his duty.

Nevins walked toward the porch. Since this man was not Callahan, it might be one of his deputies, and in that case he'd have to give himself up just as if the sheriff himself had come for him.

He wasn't surprised that Callahan had sent a deputy for him. Arresting a friend for murder was a disagreeable task. But he was resentful toward Fagin and Adams for their part in the incident, and as he walked toward the porch he was conscious of a pulse of rage.

He did not recognize the man, and he knew the two men who usually acted with Callahan when the latter thought he needed assistance.

As he came closer he discovered that he had never seen the man before, and yet the latter, having become aware of his approach, was now facing him. And glinting in the white sunlight was a nickle-plated star, ostentatiously fastened to the man's vest between the armpit and the center buttons.

A glance at the faces of the four on the porch told Nevins much. Grace Rignal was sitting motionless. Her hands were in her lap, and they were clasped so tightly that Nevins could see the muscles quivering. Her eyes were big with dread. Her face was dead white. She was breathing fast.

Nellie Porter had dropped her sewing. Her eyes were vacuous, her lips were parted. She too was pale.

Edna Pendleton sat very still. There was no color in her cheeks, but her lips were pressed firmly together. She was rigid, her hands were gripping the arms of her chair. From the glow of her eyes Nevins gathered that if she had the power she would interfere to prevent his arrest. He had her sympathy.

Seaton's face was red. He was angry, and so Nevins knew that when Seaton had told him 'it's nonsense to think that you would do a thing like that,' he had meant it. Seaton, despite his shortcomings, was ready to fight for him.

Nevins was ready to place himself in charge of the deputy. He felt that when he told Callahan about what had happened, Callahan would believe him. There was not a man in Deming, or in the entire county, for that matter, who would believe him capable of knifing a man asleep in bed. He had enemies, to be sure, but even his enemies knew him better than that!

And yet, facing the deputy, Nevins suddenly decided he would not surrender to him. In the man's eyes he saw a glint of something which should not be there had the man come merely to perform his duty as an officer of the law. There was something else in his eyes, something personal, feeling deep and intense.

He halted in front of the man, at a distance of several feet, and stood, his hands on his hips, meeting the other's eyes with level gaze.

'You wantin' somethin', stranger?' he said quietly.

'Your name Nevins?'

Nevins nodded.

'Then I'm wantin' you!' declared the man. 'Callahan wants to see you about the killin' of Watt Hamlin.'

The deputy seemed to have become oblivious of the presence of Seaton and the women on the porch. There was nothing authoritative or vainglorious in his manner, nothing of the official dignity of a representative of the law about to perform an act of duty.

His gaze did not waver from Nevins a fraction of an inch. A new light that now burned in his eyes was of a high intensity which betrayed passion.

The smile which had been on Nevins's lips had become cold, saturnine. He knew the type of man who stood before him. Callahan must have known when he sent him. There was no mistaking the significant drooping of his shoulder; no misunderstanding the light

97

in his eyes. In various parts of the country Nevins had seen men of that type—the cold, ruthless killers deliberately provoking intended victims.

This man, Nevins was certain, was not eager to arrest him. He would prefer to kill, and later report that his victim had resisted arrest.

Nevins wondered why Callahan had sent him. But while he wondered he was estimating his chances. The man undoubtedly was fast with a gun. He wouldn't be eager to force trouble if he wasn't.

But Nevins had known several killers, and he was aware that not always did they do their fighting fairly. They were not averse to taking advantages which would ensure victory for them. Only once or twice had he seen killers who had gained their reputations as such by sheer cleverness with a gun.

However, the light in the man's eyes had aroused his antagonism. And they who knew Nevins best were aware that he was never more cool and steady than when he mediated violence. Having made his decision, he smiled gravely.

'I'm figurin' on ridin' in to see Callahan tomorrow,' he said.

'You're goin' right now!' the man announced. 'With me! You're goin', dead or alive!'

It seemed to Seaton and the others on the

porch that between the two men there passed a glance which revealed the deadly purpose meditated by both of them. Never afterward could any of the watchers describe a single detail of what happened after the deputy ceased speaking.

There were a half-dozen crashes, lances of smoke and fire leaped the short space between the two men. Ballooning clouds of smoke obscured them.

Then the smoke settled. The deputy was lying, face down, on the ground at the edge of the porch. His gun was at the tips of his long fingers, a thin, blue line of smoke spiraling upward from its muzzle.

Nevins was standing rigid, his gun in hand. His left arm was dangling limply, a splotch of red stained the back of the shirt-sleeve. While Seaton and the others watched, Nevins moved forward and looked down at the deputy.

He said nothing, although a frown wrinkled his brows. When he finally turned from the deputy and faced the porch, Seaton and the others felt he had aged. But a faint, wry smile tugged at the corners of his mouth. He looked straight at Edna Pendleton.

'Well,' he said steadily, a trace of derision in his voice, 'this killin' will make this country too hot for me. From now on you'll be havin' your own way!'

# CHAPTER ELEVEN

At noon the following day Nevins again stood on the ground at the edge of the front porch. As on the preceding day, Seaton, Edna Pendleton, Grace Rignal, and Nellie Porter were there, watching him. But today the four were not sitting. Tragedy had come and gone; the body of the slain deputy had been removed. There was no visible sign that death had visited the place.

The faces that yesterday had been blanched by the imminence of a slaying were today animated by other emotions. Grace Rignal stood in the open doorway, her head drooping, her eyes glowing with regret. Nellie Porter was crying. Seaton stood near a porch column. He was rigid, his face was grim and pale.

'Well, folks,' Nevins said quietly, steadily, 'I'll be gettin' along now. Ben Gadd will be glad to tell you the things you don't know about runnin' the place.'

'Look here,' Seaton spoke gruffly. 'I think it's mighty foolish of you to run away like this. I'm a lawyer. If you say the word we'll ride over to Deming, see the sheriff, and straighten this thing out. Everybody knows that you didn't kill Watt Hamlin, and we'll all bear witness that that fool deputy brought about his own death by being too officious. Why, we all saw that he didn't want to arrest you! We'll all swear that he drew his gun before you drew yours!'

'I reckon I know what he meant to do,' said Nevins. 'But in the eyes of the law that don't change anything. You can't get around the fact that he represented the law an' that I had no right to resist him. You know that as well as I do. The law will say I killed the man it sent after me. An' I reckon I did. Things are considerably mixed, an' it seems I'm pretty well tangled up. Untanglin' wouldn't change things a lot.'

'Running away would prove your guilt,' said Seaton. 'You convict yourself.'

'A man can't be innocent when he's killed a deputy,' said Nevins. 'I reckon we can't get at it. But I'm thankin' you, Seaton.' He looked at Grace Rignal. He smiled. Gravely his gaze went to Edna Pendleton.

'So long,' he said.

He turned, walked away from the porch, went to the corral, caught his horse, saddled and bridled it, and stood beside it for a few minutes, talking with Ben Gadd, who had emerged from the stable to greet him.

Later he rode westward, not looking back. On the porch Seaton and the women watched him until distance swallowed him. And then they stood silent, for words would not come readily.

About three o'clock in the afternoon, Nevins, after crossing several miles of plain, began to ascend a long, undulating upland that led to the higher levels. Not once had he glanced backward, but his thoughts were all of the past and of those he had left on the porch of the ranch house.

He supposed he would never see any of them again. He would never be able to go back, because, as Seaton had said, his running away would prove his guilt. But his guilt would have been proved anyway. It made little difference.

He was amazed and enraged to think that Callahan had sent a killer after him. Callahan must have known what sort of man the deputy was. The sheriff's feelings toward him must have changed, and it was not until he remembered that Hamlin and Callahan had been very friendly that he found a solution of the deputy's hatred.

Once, thinking of Callahan, he drew rein and gazed southward, toward Deming. He almost yielded to a sudden impulse to ride to the town, to face Callahan. But to do so would perhaps mean another killing. He rode on again, shaking his head.

He reached the crest of the upland, wheeled his horse, and gazed back the way he had come. Objects below him were dwarfed to toylike proportions. There was no movement of any kind within the radius of his vision. The silence of centuries of desolation engulfed him. West, east, north, and south, the featureless landscape stretched. It was a dead, dun land under a white, dazzling sky. Here were space and emptiness. It all was like his future.

Which way would his fancy take him? How soon would Callahan learn of his crime and set out upon his trail? Would the sheriff organize a posse to search for him, or would he come alone?

These questions engaged his attention as he rode on, going westward. The dusk found him still in the saddle.

★     ★     ★

The Circle Dot, Edna Pendleton discovered, required little attention from her. Ben Gadd kept everything around the ranch house in order.

She had several talks with Gadd, and found him intelligent and friendly. But he was frankly worried about Nevins.

'The boss is a queer cuss,' he told Edna. 'He's quiet an' peaceable until you stir him up. An' then there ain't no tellin' what he'll do. Most of the time he's tryin' hard to hold himself in. He's got a whale of a temper!

'This here thing which has happened has got him all riled up. That there deputy was a shunk. He didn't mean to let Nevins get to

Deming. I seen that.'

'Why,' exclaimed Edna, 'I didn't see you around when Nevins was talking with the deputy!'

'Nor nobody else did,' grinned Gadd. 'But I was around, sure enough. Standin' right behind that door there.' He pointed to the stable. 'There's a sizable knot-hole in that door, an' all the time that deputy was standin' there, itchin' to go for his gun, I had a bead on him with my rifle. If he'd downed the boss he'd never have gone back to where he come from. A man can't fool me, ma'am! I've traveled some!'

'Then you really think the deputy meant to kill Nevins?'

'Shucks! There ain't no man ever needed to act like that to the boss. If that deputy had been on the level he'd have talked soft an' easy. He'd have said: "Nevins, I'm a heap sorry I got to come an' see you. I know damned well you never killed Watt Hamlin" (which would have been the Gospel truth, an' he knowed it), "but Callahan wants to see you about that killin', an' if you got time we'll ride over there."

'But what I'm gettin' at is that this thing might set the boss off. It'll be one of two ways with him. He'll go off by himself somewhere an' brood over this thing, holdin' himself in so's he won't do any more killin', or he'll break loose an' raise so much hell that it will take the whole county to down him!'

Ed Lane, Gadd told Miss Pendleton, was the Circle Dot foreman. At present Lane and the men were with the chuckwagon and most of the herd in Colter's Flat, some miles eastward. They'd stay there until the herd 'used up' the grass. No need to worry about Lane and the men. They'd take care of themselves.

Therefore, since the ranch was in such competent hands, there was little for Edna to do. But on the second morning following that upon which Nevins had departed, Ben Gadd came to the kitchen door and stuck his head in. Edna and Grace Rignal were in the kitchen.

'Ma'am,' said Gadd, 'this is the first of the month. I'm hookin' up the supply wagon to go to Deming for some things I need. I expect you'll be wantin' somethin' too?'

Edna wanted much. When Gadd drove away he was scanning a list which he considered remarkably long.

Standing on the front porch, Edna watched the wagon moving southward. Long after it disappeared over the crest of a far ridge she stood gazing in that direction.

Her thoughts were of Nevins. A feeling of deep depression had assailed her after she had seen Nevins ride away. Her cheeks grew pale as she now thought of him.

She wondered why she had ever thought

she hated him. For since she had learned more about him she had discovered that she liked him. He had temper, to be sure. She had plenty of that herself. And toward both her and Seaton he had exhibited flashes of contempt. But the contempt, she now realized, had been justified by her actions and manner and by Seaton's.

She stood, oblivious of her surroundings, enveloped in the brooding calm of the morning. She no longer saw the vast land that stretched before her. She was mentally reviewing the scene that day in Nevins's office when he had given her a copy of the partnership agreement between himself and her father. She was seeing Nevins again as his action had revealed him. She could still see the oddly ironic light in his eyes as he had watched her. She saw that light change as he continued to watch; she observed the new expression that had leaped into his eyes—the dawning of admiration, an entirely new understanding of her character.

So absorbed was she in her mental picture that she did not hear the clattering of hoofs near the porch. But when a voice reached her ears she turned swiftly, to see Fagin and Adams sitting on their horses at the edge of the porch.

It was Fagin's voice she had heard. There had been a laugh in it.

'Must be somethin' mighty interestin',' he

said.

'Yes,' she answered, facing the two men. 'It is the wagon going to Deming for supplies.'

'Sure,' he said, 'we seen the wagon goin'. That was Ben Gadd drivin', wasn't it?'

Edna nodded.

'An' there was someone with him. We was so far away that we couldn't just make out who it was.'

'Mr. Seaton was with him.'

Fagin turned in the saddle and deliberately scrutinized the land in the vicinity of the ranch house. His slow gaze went to the stable, the mess and bunkhouse, and the other buildings.

'Boys all gone?' he asked.

'Ed Lane and the other men are in Colter's Flat,' Edna told him.

'You an' Grace Rignal here alone?'

'There is Nellie Porter,' Edna informed him.

'Why, sure enough!' He grinned widely at the child, who averted her gaze, although she had been watching him steadily.

'Well,' he remarked, again looking at Edna, 'we was passin' here an' thought we'd stop and say "hello."'

'That was thoughtful of you,' she said, smiling. 'Won't you get down and rest?'

'We was thinkin' of it,' Fagin agreed. He looked at Adams. Both grinned and dismounted.

Fagin reached the porch first and stood grinning, watching Edna. Adams stepped up on the edge of the porch and placed a hand on one of the porch columns. He stood watching Fagin and Edna. His face was expressionless.

'You like it here?' asked Fagin.

'Very much.'

'You're figurin' to stay, of course?'

'I think I shall.'

'Got everything all settled with Nevins?'

Reluctantly Edna replied that she had settled her affairs with Nevins. She couldn't understand such frank interest in her affairs, nor the motive that prompted such interest; and she felt they were unpardonably curious.

Yet she supposed such behavior was the custom of the country.

'You didn't have no trouble with Nevins?'

'Not a bit of trouble.'

A shadow of disappointment passed over Fagin's face.

'That's good,' he said. 'We figured you would have, an' we'd decided we'd help you out. Me an' Brandt Adams know somethin' about the deal your dad made with Nevins.'

Edna thought Fagin's statement sounded vindictive.

'Where's Nevins now?' asked Fagin after a short silence.

'Mr. Nevins went away the day before yesterday,' answered Edna.

'Ha!' ejaculated Fagin. He winked at Adams, then again looked at Edna.

'Where did he go to?' he asked.

'I think he has left the country,' replied Edna.

Fagin's mouth opened at the information. He stared hard.

'Didn't Callahan's deputy take him to Deming?' he queried. 'When we give Callahan Nevins's knife an' told him what Nevins had done, he said he was sendin' one of his deputies, a guy named Logan, after Nevins. An' Logan ain't the man to let anybody get away from him. I reckon Logan is gone after Nevins?'

'No,' said Edna. 'I think not. Most certainly not. For, you see, they—Mr. Nevins and the deputy—had words right here beside the porch. The deputy was insulting. I—I think he wanted to provoke Nevins to draw his gun. In fact, I am willing to swear that such was his intention.'

'An' did Nevins pull it?' questioned Fagin. His eyes were big, bright, full of morbid interest.

'Yes, he drew it,' answered Edna.

Fagin drew a deep breath.

'Nevins lit out,' he said. 'Where's Logan?'

Edna shuddered. 'Mr. Nevins and Ben Gadd buried him,' she answered.

'Hell's fire!' exclaimed Fagin. He was on his feet. Adams had got up too.

'Nevins killed Logan?' Fagin almost shouted at Edna.

'Right where you are standing,' Edna told him. She took a malicious satisfaction in observing how the men received her news.

Fagin stood staring at Edna. She had given him a start, but he was slowly recovering. He squinted his eyes at her and at last smiled crookedly.

'An' Nevins has left the country,' he said. 'Does he figure on comin' back?'

'I think not. The deputy had come to arrest him. He was an officer of the law. Would you come back?'

Fagin again squinted at her.

'You're right,' he said; 'I wouldn't.'

He sat down again. Adams did likewise. Fagin clasped his hands about a knee and leaned back against a porch column.

'Well,' he said, 'that's how she shapes up, eh? It's funny, ain't it, Brandt, damned funny!'

Both men laughed.

'What is funny?' questioned Edna. Her voice was quiet and steady, and yet through her ran a sudden chill of apprehension.

'What's been happenin' is mighty funny,' returned Fagin, grinning.

'I can't see anything funny about it!' declared Edna. 'And I don't feel a bit like laughing!'

'You wouldn't. But look at it a little

different. There's Porter an' his wife. The Indians got them. He left a heap of stuff—cattle an' such. There's Watt Hamlin. He cashes in, leavin' his wife an' more cattle an' stuff. There's Ross Nevins, killin' Logan, an' charged with killin' Hamlin. He's had to light out of the country. He won't come back. That makes him as good as dead. An' here's me an' Brandt Adams, which has got to take charge of things for all of the unfortunate folks an' keep things runnin'.'

'You don't mean that you intend to take over the management of the Circle Dot?' asked Edna.

'Yep. We can't stand around an' see you an' that tenderfoot dude ruin things.' He looked at Adams. 'We've always had a soft spot for the Circle Dot, ain't we, Brandt?'

'For quite a while,' agreed Adams.

'Well,' said Edna, 'I warn you not to attempt to interfere with the Circle Dot.'

'You're warnin' us, eh?'

Fagin got up and stood on the edge of the porch. There had come a sudden change in his manner. There was a confidence in him that she had not seen before; he was calmly triumphant.

He moved close to her and stood, his arms folded over his chest, smiling at her.

'You're warnin' us, eh?' he repeated. 'Well, I reckon we ain't none disturbed over what you think. An' you warnin' us don't bother us

111

any. Especially me. I'm goin' to have my say around here. For ever since Ross Nevins killed Watt Hamlin I've been worryin' about what would become of his interest in the Circle Dot. A fool woman might sell him out; she might ruin the place; or she might squander it, You never can tell.

'As I say, I was worried. An' so yesterday I went over to see Judge Travis, at Willets. I told him what had been happenin', an' what I was afraid of. An' so he appointed me administrator of Nevins's interest. An' I'm here to take hold.'

Edna's first emotion was amazement. Indignation succeeded the amazement.

'Why,' she exclaimed, 'that is preposterous!'

'Mebbe,' he said. He reached into a pocket and drew out a legal-looking paper which he unfolded and shoved toward her. Leaning forward a little, she read.

The paper was a court document confirming Fagin's statement. At the bottom of the paper was Judge Travis's signature.

Edna stepped back after reading. Fagin was enjoying her discomfiture.

'That settles that question, I reckon,' he said. 'I'm stayin' right here on the job. I'll be usin' Nevins's room. But we ain't through yet. Adams has got another court order which he wants to show you. It's about Nellie Porter. Judge Travis is some worried that

Nellie Porter ain't in proper company, I reckon, so he's ordered Adams to bring her over to his place.'

Again Edna found herself reading from a legal-looking paper which Fagin thrust toward her. Out of the stilted phrasing of the words written there she gathered that Brandt Adams had been appointed administrator of the Porter property and guardian of Nellie Porter until the girl should reach maturity. Appended to the document was another specifically commanding Edna Pendleton and Robert M. Nevins to deliver Nellie Porter to the guardianship of Adams.

Edna stood dismayed, uncertain of her impulses. In her, because of the traditions of her kind, was respect of the law. But at this moment there seethed in her a scorn for the law that would permit a man like Fagin—or Adams—to exercise any control whatever over an unprotected girl or woman. She stepped back from Fagin.

'You shan't have her!' she declared. 'I don't care whether you have the law back of you or not. If Judge Travis wants Nellie Porter, let him send an officer after her. She shall not leave this house!'

Fagin laughed. He moved toward her, and when she perceived the expression in his eyes she turned and ran toward the doorway.

She almost ran into the muzzle of a rifle which suddenly appeared in the doorway.

Behind the rifle was Grace Rignal. The muzzle of the weapon was directed at Fagin's chest, and he cursed as he halted.

'Damn your hide, what are you interferin' for?' he demanded. 'You drop that gun an' mind your own business!'

'Don't move another step, Fagin!' warned Grace. 'Nellie,' she added, speaking to the child, who was already sidling along the porch toward her, 'come into the house, please!'

Fagin had been retreating from the leveled rifle. It seemed to Grace that she was to have an easy victory, and she took another step forward in order to discover the whereabouts of Adams, who had vanished with her first word to Fagin.

She didn't see Adams, and for an instant her gaze wavered. Simultaneously Adams leaped. He had been creeping along the wall of the house toward her.

The rifle went off, but the bullet was harmlessly buried in the porch floor a little to one side of Fagin. Grace caught a glimpse of Fagin's face. The rifle was twisted from her grasp and she was violently shoved against one of the door-jambs.

Adams unloaded the rifle and threw it to the ground at the edge of the porch.

'No respect for the law, eh?' he said. 'Well, there's ways of learnin' folks to respect it!'

Furiously Grace slapped the grinning face

that he stuck close to hers. His eyes malignant, his lips blaspheming, Adams seized her by the throat. With a ferocity that terrified her, he forced her head back against the door-jamb.

Grace saw Fagin leap. She heard him curse, saw one of his arms encircle Adams's neck as he pulled the latter away.

'You damned fool!' Fagin said. 'Ain't you got no sense at all?'

Adams's frenzy seemed to pass as quickly as it had seized him. He stood at a little distance from Grace, smiling wanly, his face pale, his breath coming fast. He looked like an animal driven from its kill, though even as Grace watched him flecks of returning reason glinted in his eyes. He seemed to shrink a little from the passion in Fagin's eyes, and he silently obeyed Fagin's curt order: 'Get the kid an' drag it!'

Nellie Porter screamed when Adams seized her, and held out her arms imploringly to the girls as Adams threw her upon one of the horses, mounted behind her, and sent the animal scampering away.

Both girls leaped off the porch in a vain effort to interfere. And then they stood gazing helplessly at each other as Adams and his captive vanished into the western distance.

Fagin grinned at them as they returned to the porch.

'There ain't no use fightin', ladies,' he said.

'Things is goin' to change considerable around here!'

## CHAPTER TWELVE

Shortly after midnight of the first day of Fagin's brutal assumption of authority at the Circle Dot, Edna softly opened the door of her room and gazed down the narrow hall, which was faintly illuminated by a bracket lamp at the far end.

She stood in the partly opened door for some minutes, listening, hearing nothing.

Fagin had carried out his expressed determination to occupy Nevins's room. Both Grace and Edna had gone upstairs early to avoid Fagin, and both were occupying the room that Grace had given Edna on the night of the latter's arrival.

Neither girl had undressed. And now, as Edna stood in the partly opened doorway listening for any sound which would tell her that Fagin was still about, Grace was standing breathlessly behind her.

Both girls were pale. But in the faint light from the bracket lamp Grace's eyes held only a sullen resentment, while Edna's were agleam with determination. Grace appeared to be willing to wait for the day of Fagin's punishment, while Edna, finding inaction

116

intolerable, meant to hasten it.

After listening for a time, Edna stepped out into the hall. She was arrayed in riding togs that she had brought with her. Her light boots, soft and pliable, made no sound as she moved down the hall to the stairway, Grace following her. Grace wore only a house dress, but in her right hand dangled a heavy revolver.

They slipped down the stairs noiselessly, gained the big living room, opened the door and passed out to the porch. They went directly to the stable, where Grace took down a saddle, a bridle, and a rope. These they carried out and placed on a top rail of the corral fence. Then, as silently as possible, Grace roped a horse, led it to the corral gates, saddled and bridled it, and helped Edna to mount.

'It is right straight west,' directed Grace, pointing into the moonlit land. 'After you reach the crest of that first big rise you will strike the trail. It is almost a wagon road, and you won't be in any danger of losing it until you get within two miles of Willets, where there is a stretch of broken country.

'But if you lose it there, you must keep right on, going as straight as you can, and you'll run right into Willets. Judge Travis lives in a big white house on your right just at the edge of town. Goodbye, and don't be afraid for me. If Fagin gets fresh I'll shoot him!'

Edna rose westward, with the moon swimming almost overhead. When she reached the crest of the first rise she turned in the saddle and looked back. She could dimly make out Grace's figure, still at the corral gate. Then she rode down the farther slope of the rise into a strange and ghostly world.

She intended to go straight to Judge Travis. She was worried about Nellie Porter, and convinced that Judge Travis could have no real knowledge of the characters of Fagin and Adams, or he would not have endowed them with so much authority.

With Edna's respect for the law there was also awe and reverence for the men who dispensed justice. She felt that she had only to acquaint Judge Travis with the facts to induce him to countermand the order he had given Adams regarding the guardianship of the Porter girl.

And she was assured that when she told the judge about Nevins's predicament he would hasten to withdraw Fagin from the Circle Dot. She would give a bond, if necessary, as an assurance that she would properly conduct the Circle Dot.

She had questioned Grace about Judge Travis and had learned that Travis was honored and respected in the country. He was implacable and relentless toward all doers of evil. He had been reelected time after time.

He was dignified, fearless, and yet kindly.

Edna had tried to induce Grace to accompany her to Judge Travis's house, but Grace had chosen to stay at the Circle Dot. She wasn't afraid of Fagin, she had said. Fagin was smarter than Adams, and not so much like an animal. He'd be autocratic, perhaps, and would never use physical force to accomplish his aims.

Edna rode steadily, eagerly for several hours.

She felt the darkness had swallowed her. She could no longer see the trail. Far away, eastward, she could see the moonlight touching the peaks of some mountains, but ahead of her was an impenetrable black gulf.

Grimly she rode into it, although she made no attempt to guide the horse. She rode him carefully, with a good grip on the reins and her knees pressing his sides. If he stumbled and fell she meant to stay with him, for she knew that if he fell and she were to tumble out of the saddle, she could never find him again. She didn't care to travel through that country on foot.

She sat trembling when the horse suddenly halted. For a few moments she was in a frenzy of fear and dread, for she thought of robbers and other evil riders, and she shrank in the saddle, expecting each instant to hear a gruff voice or feel hands clutching at her. When there came no sound or movement around her she sighed audibly with relief. And then she remembered having read tales of horses halting of their own volition upon approaching dangerous spots such as cliffs and ditches, and she endeavoured to penetrate the blackness ahead of her in an effort to see what obstructed.

She could see nothing. She was assailed with a sensation of futility, of helplessness. She did not dare urge the horse onward for fear of a catastrophe, and so she continued to sit, vacillating, uncertain.

She leaned forward, resting her hands upon the high pommel of the saddle. The movement took her head forward a little, and a glimmer of light, like a pinpoint in the vast darkness, flashed in her eyes. She turned quickly to face the pinpoint. It was to her left, and so far away that at first it appeared to be a low-hanging star.

But it was too low for a star. It was, in fact, lower than the ground upon which her horse stood. And so she finally decided it was down in a valley.

A house was there, probably, and perhaps the light shone through a window. Possibly the presence of the light explained the action of the horse in halting. The animal, unguided, had been uncertain of her destination, and was awaiting her pleasure.

There probably was a trail leading toward the light; the horse must have seen it. She didn't know if there was still a trail stretching out ahead of her. If she had reached the edge of the broken country about which Grace had warned her, there would be no trail westward, and she ought to ride straight ahead.

The trouble was that she didn't know whether she had been riding straight or not. It was quite possible that she might have been riding off at an angle for some little time, for since the moon went down she hadn't been able to see anything.

Of course, the horse would follow the trail as long as there was a trail, but the point was that he might have passed the end of the trail some time ago. It might even be possible that the light she saw was one of the lights of Willets.

She looked back. Blackness. There was nothing by which she could establish a sense of direction, and as she continued to speculate she began to have a feeling that she would be doing wrong to urge the horse. Left alone, he would probably take her straight to Willets, whereas if she attempted to guide him she might get lost or go plunging down a precipice.

Obeying a sudden impulse, she gently struck the animal with the quirt she carried. Instantly the horse swerved, lunged, and galloped toward the light.

She was almost satisfied now, and she

watched with interest as the light grew larger in her vision. The farther she rode the firmer became her conviction that the light was in Willets, and that she would have been foolish to reject the wisdom of the animal she rode.

She rode for half an hour, while the light drew closer and she tried to distinguish its character. After a while she decided it was rectangular and was therefore coming through a window or a door. When she drew near enough to perceive that it was shining through a window, she found herself in a dense wood, for light beams from the window shone on the branches and leaves of trees.

Deep in the woods she halted the horse and sat motionless in the saddle, listening, peering about her.

If the light came from a window of a house in Willets, why weren't there more lights? This interrogation was, she felt, founded upon her fear that this might not be Willets after all. Willets must be a little town, and it would not be odd that in such a place only one house should be illuminated. It was more astonishing that at this hour there should be any light at all!

At the thought she grew apprehensive, and she tried hard to detect the outlines of other buildings. When she failed she resolutely closed her lips, took up the reins, and urged the horse forward until she reached a point at the edge of the wood where a tall brush grew.

The brush screened her, and she sat there for some time with all her senses alert, trying to detect the unusual.

The house was now outlined to her against a background of star haze that had a greenish-yellow, phosphorous light, and she observed that the structure was a one-story affair with a low, flat roof. It had, she felt, only two rooms. One was dark, while the light she had been seeing shone through a window of the other.

There was a low, rambling porch across the front of the house, which faced eastward, and she could distinguish the slender, crooked poles which, answering as columns, supported the roof. Behind the house she could see the dim tracery of a fence. From a point off to her right she could hear a calf bleating. In the wood behind her were the indescribable noises of the timber denizens; to her ears from a distance came the shrill barking of coyotes.

She was frightened. She sat fighting an impulse to wheel her horse and return to the Circle Dot. At this instant she regretted starting on the trip when she had. She might have waited until the dawn, though she knew that if she had waited Fagin would not have permitted her to leave.

By concentrating her thoughts upon Nellie Porter she succeeded in conquering her fear, and at last she dismounted, trailed the reins over the head of the horse, and walked toward the house. She felt she was now lost—unless this house was in Willets—but she did not intend to reveal herself to the inhabitants of the dwelling until she made an effort to discover what kind of people they were.

She moved to the rear of the building until she reached a wall. Making her way stealthily along the wall, she reached the window through which the light came. A bush with heavy foliage grew beside the window, and screened by that she peered into the room.

The light came from a kerosene lamp upon a big, rough table near the center of the room. A man sat on one corner of the table. One of his legs was drawn under him, the other dangled almost to the floor. He was facing the window through which Edna was watching.

His left arm was bent across his chest, the hand caught under the right armpit; the right arm was crooked at the elbow, the forearm perpendicular, the hand was at his chin, and a thumb and forefinger were engaged in pressing his lower lip, the finger on one side, the thumb on the other.

The man's gaze seemed to be fixed directly on the window at which Edna was watching, and she quickly dodged back, fearful that he had seen her. But when after an interval she heard no sound she looked again, to see that he was still sitting in the same position, his gaze still on the window.

He was in deep thought. His gaze was introspective, and he did not see the window at which he appeared to be looking.

He was tall, handsome, distinguished. His complexion was that which Edna had heard described as 'sandy'. He had a good chin, a broad forehead, a nose of the type known as Grecian. Edna thought his mouth was a trifle large and his lips a little too full.

But his hair interested her; his hair and his eyes. The eyes were dreamy, although big and clear. They were the eyes of a poet or a lazy man. They lacked the keen hardness of the alert captain of business, and yet they had fire in them, the fire of deep, intense thought. Also, they held a glint of recklessness. Just now the man was lost in thought, but Edna felt that when roused he must be a commanding figure.

His hair was a rich dark red. It was wavy and abundant. His age Edna felt she was not competent to determine, though she was certain he could not be more than thirty.

There was a knife-sheath in the left leg of the chaps. His broad-brimmed hat lay on the table beside him.

There was another man in the room seated on a chair at the table. He was of medium height and dark. His black hair was long and straight, his nose thin and drooping, his mouth large, the lips thin and loose. His chin receded slightly, and his neck where it was exposed by the open collar of his shirt was scrawny and corded. His eyes were black, lambent, roving. At the instant Edna looked at him he was grinning up into the face of the red-haired man.

'Well, then,' he said, 'I reckon she's all shaped up?'

The window was open; the man's voice was clear and distinct. The red-haired man smiled.

'Looks that way,' he answered.

'But look here, chief,' continued the dark man, 'suppose the soldiers find out about that Indian deal?'

The red-haired man laughed. The laugh was deep, rich, vibrant.

'That's likely, isn't it, Naylor?' he scoffed. 'It seems to me Fagin and Adams reported there weren't any Indians left to do any talking. You were there yourself, weren't you?' he charged, swinging round. 'You saw to that, didn't you?'

Naylor seemed to cringe under the accusation in the red-haired man's voice. He flushed, stammered:

'Sure. There wasn't—there couldn't none of them hev got away. But you can't always tell. Mebbe them redskins that busted away from the reservation had talked to some of their friends before they left. An' thet damned major over to Fort Bayard is just nosey enough to go smellin' around.'

The chief laughed again. 'They couldn't possibly find anything to it other than just another uprising. Don't get uneasy, Naylor.'

'Well, then,' said Naylor, 'if thet's all set, when we goin' to begin on them herds?'

'We're not going to be in a hurry about that,' replied the chief. 'Haste right now would bring suspicion upon us. We've got to have patience. There's a lot of cattle to dispose of. Fagin estimates there are more than six thousand head at the Circle Dot. Porter had upward of fifteen hundred, though they are pretty well scattered. Hamlin must have had a couple of thousand. That's about ten thousand, roughly.

'We can drive some to Deming. We'll get others over to Rincon. We'll have to do it slow and easy.' He paused meditatively, and his eyes were gleaming with a light so soft and tender that Edna, intently watching them, found it hard to believe that she had only just now heard him convict himself of knowledge of the terrible crime of permitting a massacre.

She stood, her knees knocking together, fascinated, paralysed. She could not have moved from the window if she had known that the next instant he would discover her.

'I don't want any of you boys to go near the Circle Dot. Fagin can take care of that,' resumed the chief.

Naylor smirked slyly.

'She's a thoroughbred, chief,' he said.

'Meaning Miss Pendleton,' returned the other. His eyes were glowing. 'Yes, she's beautiful,' he added. 'I saw her in Deming the day she arrived.' He laughed. 'It's too damned bad Matt Blandell didn't succeed in hanging that fool dude who came here with her!'

'Haw, haw, haw!' laughed Naylor; 'thet sure was a mighty close shave for thet dude! An' Matt thinkin' he was hangin' Ross Nevins!' His eyes grew vindictive. 'But anyhow, Matt got Hamlin. She worked out pretty good!' he exulted.

'But not good enough,' said the chief. 'Adams says Nevins beat Logan to the draw.'

'Killed him?'

'Yes. I told Logan to be careful. Nevins is lightning with a gun.'

'Whar's Nevins now?'

'Nobody knows. None of the boys have seen him since he left the Circle Dot. We've got to get him some way. He's bad medicine when he's aroused!'

Naylor pursed his lips, frowned.

The red-haired man slipped off the table, stood up, and yawned. He was tall and muscular, and there was a smooth, animallike ease in his movement.

'Well,' he said, 'bed suits me. We've ridden quite a distance tonight.'

'Fifty miles if we rode a foot,' confirmed

Naylor. 'I'm kind of fagged out myself.'

Edna drew away from the window. She was reeling dizzily when she made her way to the edge of the wood where she had left her horse, and when she reached the animal she leaned against it and clutched the high pommel of the saddle to support herself.

Although she was aware of her danger, she lacked the strength to climb into the saddle. For she had thought the incidents of the last few days were those unrelated happenings which occasionally mar the quiet peacefulness of everyday life—tragedies which are the result of passion.

Now she had discovered that behind all the tragedy was sinister purpose, comprehensive scheming and ruthless force. The red-haired man, Naylor, Fagin, Adams, and a number of other men, were in league against Nevins, Hamlin's wife, Nellie Porter, and herself. They would rob and murder to attain their aims.

Somehow she got on the back of the horse, wheeled him and sent him plunging into the night.


## CHAPTER THIRTEEN

When the dawn came, Edna was sitting upon her horse in the center of a vast section of wild, virgin country, straining her eyes in an effort to distinguish a trail.

She was lost. She had passed the Willets trail in the darkness, for her only thought when riding away from the cabin had been to place as great a distance as possible between herself and the red-haired man.

The section which was disclosed to her by the first streaks of dawn was desolate and trackless. No trail crossed it.

But although she was lost, she was slowly recovering from the horror of the night's revelation, and her determination to go to Judge Travis was unshaken. She meant to tell him what she had heard, and after telling him she would demand the protection of the law.

When she perceived that the grey streak of light on the horizon was widening, she recovered her sense of direction. She headed the horse away from the growing light and sent him against the upland. And when she was at last riding the level land of a high mesa, she again found the Willets trail.

An hour later she was in the section of broken country about which Grace Rignal had warned her. But she was confident now, and although she slowed her horse and rode carefully, she went on steadily until the broken stretch was behind and she saw Willets directly in front of her.

Willets, she felt, hardly deserved the dignity of a name. It was a collection of shanties and stores huddled together on a level near a small river. The doors of the stores were closed when she rode down the dusty street; there was no one in sight. A dog barked at her sharply and then subsided.

When she came to a large white house at the farther edge of the town she felt sure, from Grace's description, that Judge Travis occupied it, and so she rode boldly to the front porch, dismounted, and knocked on the front door.

After a short wait she heard footsteps inside. The door creaked, opened a trifle, and a thin-faced woman looked out at her.

'The jedge?' she queried, answering Edna's question. 'Well, yes, I reckon he's here. But he left word he wasn't to be disturbed early. You'd better go along an' come back after a while. The jedge ain't no early riser.'

Edna smiled.

'It is early, isn't it?' she said. 'I hadn't thought of that. But won't you tell him that I'll take just a minute of his time?'

'Huh. Well, I'll see.'

There followed a five-minutes interval in which Edna stood scanning the featureless country surrounding the town. She was on the point of deciding that the thin-faced woman had no intention of waking Judge Travis, when she heard a sound inside the house.

The sound was that of a footstep on a bare

131

floor. It was heavy. Edna thought of a boot heel. And she somehow got the impression that the owner of the boots was irritated.

But she wasn't dismayed at that. She was resolved that justice should be done, and she faced the door eagerly.

The door opened and a man's head appeared. The hair was tousled; the man's eyes were blinking, and they held an expression of irritation, just as Edna expected.

She had been conning over the words of her opening sentence, and she knew just what she had intended to say to the judge. But she stood there speechless, dazed, bewildered, her brain reeling with amazement as the man spoke brusquely:

'I'm Judge Travis. What can I do for you?'

For the man, despite his tousled hair and his blinking eyes, and the fact that he was in Willets when she thought he was sleeping at a certain cabin miles eastward, was the red-haired man whom Naylor had addressed as 'chief'!

★　　　★　　　★

Edna Pendleton had not acquired the slightly arrogant manner which had antagonized Nevins without gaining in addition the ability to control her emotions. Therefore, although the revelation of the red-haired man's identity

132

had thrown her into confusion, she succeeded in disguising her feelings.

Her wide-eyed amazement became self-deprecation, and her dismay seemed merely natural feminine shyness to Judge Travis, whose eyes were no longer blinking, but were now gleaming with bold admiration.

'I am Judge Travis,' he said. 'What can I do for you?'

Although, since Edna had overheard Travis and Naylor talking, she was aware that she could hope for no assistance from the man who stood before her, she felt that she must go ahead just as if she had no knowledge of his real character. She must dissemble, she must not let him suspect that she knew of his scheme to rob and murder several of the inhabitants of the section.

'I am Edna Pendleton, of the Circle Dot,' she said quietly, although inwardly she was yearning to tell him that she was aware of his despicable character, and that she hated him because of the light in his eyes at that minute, a light which expressed avid interest, 'and I have come here to talk to you about Nellie Porter.'

'I'm glad to make your acquaintance, Miss Pendleton,' the judge rejoined. 'Come in, if you will excuse my appearance. We can talk better.'

She entered as he stepped back and held the door open for her. She did not take the chair he motioned to, but stood just inside the door—which he closed—watching him and wondering how any man could be so hypocritical. For she felt that if she had not possessed knowledge of his real character she would never have suspected him capable of doing the things he had done.

He appeared to her, as he stood there smiling, an entirely different person than he had seemed last night in the cabin when talking with Naylor. There was a dignity in his manner which even his tousled appearance did not affect; a judicial atmosphere, which transcended mere clothing, surrounded him.

He was so magnetic a personality that a quaver of apprehension swept over Edna as she watched him, a fear that he would win her admiration in spite of what she knew about him.

'Won't you take a chair?' he asked.

'No, thank you. My business won't take long. I merely want to ask you to rescind your order appointing Brandt Adams guardian over Nellie Porter.'

'So Adams has visited the Circle Dot? Why do you object to Adams as guardian for Nellie Porter?'

'In my opinion he is not qualified to act as guardian of a young girl.'

'What makes you think so, Miss Pendleton?'

'He isn't a gentleman,' answered Edna.

'Ah!' smiled the judge.

The smile exasperated Edna.

'He is a brute!' she declared. And then she related what had happened on the porch in the Circle Dot ranch house when Fagin and Adams had demanded the custody of Nellie Porter.

'Adams and Fagin were acting with full authority, Miss Pendleton. It seems to me that you were the one at fault. Don't you know that you were obstructing an officer of the court in the performance of his duty?'

Edna momentarily lost her temper. The thought that Travis could stand there and defend Adams and Fagin when she knew he was as guilty as they, and she not able to tell him so, enraged her. She felt she must let him know that she had a suspicion of the work the men were engaged in.

She told Travis of the conversation she had overheard in Deming, hinging upon the question of a Two Diamond cow. Nevins, it had seemed to her, had suspected Adams and Fagin of doing something they should not have done.

Travis laughed easily, smoothly. 'Nevins didn't make any specific charge, then?' he asked.

'No; but it was easy to understand that Nevins suspected them of stealing!' declared Edna.

'And would you want me to condemn

135

Adams because Nevins suspected him?' asked Travis.

'Yes!' she answered. 'Because Mr. Nevins is an honest man!'

'A woman's reason, Miss Pendleton. A woman's judgment.' There was a mocking glint in his eyes. 'Women are constitutionally and notoriously inaccurate in their judgment of men, Miss Pendleton,' he announced slowly. 'And I feel that you have based your judgment upon appearances.' He laughed as if deeply amused. 'Adams isn't much to look at, for a fact,' he added, 'while Nevins is of a type to attract women.'

Edna felt her composure going. She no longer saw Travis as a judge; the dignity she had detected in his appearance had vanished. She was seeing him now as Fagin's chief; a sinister, wanton figure of evil. The smile on his lips aroused in her a turgid fury.

Her rage conquered her. She felt she must drive the mocking smile from his lips. And so, with her voice cold from the scorn and contempt that filled her, she told him what she had seen the night before while looking into the cabin window.

When, breathless, she finished, she realized that she had made a mistake. The only apparent effect her words had upon him was to change the character of his smile. It was now twisting, speculative.

'So you heard that, eh?' he said. 'You

136

didn't miss a word of it?'

'And that is why you appointed Fagin and Adams!' she declared.

'Yes,' he admitted. He was watching her intently.

'And now that you know these things, what do you intend doing?' he added slowly, quietly.

'I intend to ride straight to Deming and tell Sheriff Callahan what I have discovered!'

'You recognized me when I opened the door,' he said. 'You pretended you didn't. Why?'

'I—I thought perhaps I had made a mistake.'

'No, that isn't the explanation,' he said. 'You were startled, afraid. You talked to gain time to get your thoughts together. You intended to go to Callahan just as soon as you could get out of here without arousing my suspicions. Why didn't you keep quiet? You might have got away with it.' He grinned when she reddened. 'Temper, eh?' he mocked.

She was silent, watching him.

'Too much temper is a bad thing,' he went on. 'Yours has got you into trouble. A great deal of trouble, I think. You see, you know too much about me, and if you went to Callahan with your story there would be an investigation in which the soldiers from Fort Bayard would take a hand. That would make things very uncomfortable for me. I shall have to take measures to keep you from talking.'

Edna's face had whitened. Yet she faced him courageously, defiantly.

'I shall talk just as soon as I can get to Sheriff Callahan!' she declared.

'Ah!' he said softly, 'that's just it. Therefore you will never reach Callahan.'

She moved toward the door, and to her vast amazement, considering the threat of his words and manner, he made no move to stop her. He stood watching her, his eyes narrowed and gleaming. And when she opened the door and stood for an instant in the opening looking back at him, still amazed, he shook his head negatively.

'No,' he said, 'there won't be any struggle in the doorway. Did you expect it? My dear girl, I couldn't keep you here. You ride right along to Deming. It's quite a distance. About a hundred miles. But don't waste any time telling your story to anybody in Willets. These people here are my friends.'

He stood in the doorway watching her as she mounted, and rode away.

Thoroughly frightened by contemplation of the distance she must ride to reach the Circle Dot or Deming, and by the enigma of Travis's manner, she rode a few miles at breakneck speed. The trail led downward in a long, gradual slope, and when she reached the edge of a broad level at the bottom of the slope she looked back.

And when at the edge of town she saw a horse and rider coming toward her, she gave the animal under her his head and fled recklessly into the yawning distance that stretched before her.

## CHAPTER FOURTEEN

Before Edna had ridden a mile she knew she had made her second mistake of the morning. The horse she rode had been traveling since midnight the night before, and in that time had had neither feed nor water, and the terrific pace at which he had traveled the mile after she had sighted the horseman at the edge of Willets had winded him. She heard his breath coming in shrill wheezes, and she despairingly searched for a covert in which she might hide in an effort to throw the horseman off her trail.

But there was no covert. The level was featureless except for clumps of cactus growing here and there. Far away to her left was a line of timber, but the horseman had kept in sight of her and she knew she would not be able to escape in that direction.

So, clenching her teeth determinedly, she lashed the horse with the quirt she carried.

The action drew a burst of speed out of the animal, but presently he began to falter again, and despite all her urging the pace grew slower and slower.

Meantime the pursuing horseman came on at a pace that now seemed leisurely. It appeared to Edna that he was enjoying her plight and, there being no danger of interference, was permitting her to ride until the horse would carry her no farther.

Once, when the horse stumbled and halted, to stand with its legs braced while it shrilled breath into its lungs, the horseman also halted and sat motionless in the saddle watching her. He was, she estimated, perhaps a half-mile distant.

Later, when her horse went on again, the rider followed. In a shallow arroyo which descended to a gully her animal again halted. This time, having reached the end of the level land, she could not see the horseman immediately.

But after a short interval, just when she was meditating deserting the horse and taking to foot in an effort to seek concealment in some wild brush that grew at the bottom of the gully, she saw the horseman appear on the edge of the plain above.

Again he halted and watched her. He was not more than a few hundred feet distant now, and she got a good view of his face. The horseman was Naylor, the man who had been with Travis in the cabin the night before.

Somehow she didn't fear Naylor. Naylor was under orders, and the fact that he so far hadn't attempted to molest her indicated that he didn't intend violence. Naylor had been sent to capture her.

There was little doubt of his ability to do that, and it appeared to her that he was merely waiting for her to reach a certain point before he attempted it.

She got her horse going again. She rode him down into the gully, and through the place until she reached a stream of water that intersected it. The animal refused to go farther. He halted at the bank of the stream, plunged his muzzle into the water, and drank.

Naylor rode close and sat in the saddle watching. Edna did not look at him, although she had heard him approach.

'I reckon he'll founder hisself, ma'am,' he said.

'Oh!' she exclaimed scornfully. 'So you are here! Perhaps you will be good enough to tell me why you have been following me?'

'I reckon there's no secret about that, ma'am. Travis was tellin' me to follow you.'

'For what reason?'

'He was sayin' you knowed somethin' an' that you wasn't to get to Deming or the Circle Dot.'

'The beast!'

141

Naylor was silent. He appeared reluctant and apologetic, although sullenly determined.

Edna said no more to him just then. While her horse was still drinking she slid out of the saddle and darted toward the wild brush that fringed the sloping side of the gully. She had taken only a dozen steps when she heard a swishing over her head and a noose settled down over her shoulders, pinned her arms to her sides, and brought her to a sudden halt.

Silently she fought to free herself. But the more she struggled the tighter grew the rope. She saw Naylor's horse backing, keeping the rope taut. The range-bred animal would permit her to get no slack in the rope. Naylor slid to the ground and leaped toward her. She kicked viciously at him, but missed.

And then, in spite of her furious resistance, Naylor tied her hands behind her with a piece of 'hogging' rope. Next, while she still silently struggled, he picked her up bodily and carried her to his horse. He placed her in the saddle and swung up behind her. Without a word he took up the reins and sent the horse down the gully at a fair rate of speed.

Edna was too furiously angry to talk, and Naylor was in no mood to say anything. They went on silently.

Within half an hour from the time she had felt the noose settle over her shoulders Edna was riding a trail which seemed familiar. But it was not until she saw a cabin ahead of her that she realized Naylor was taking her to the place where the night before she had seen him and Travis through a window.

Once more, when Naylor dismounted and lifted her down, she tried to escape. This time Naylor lost patience with her. He leaped after her, seized her roughly, and growled:

'Damn you! if you try that again I'll truss you!'

Naylor carried her into the cabin and placed her in a chair.

'Now, if you know what's best for you, you'll stay where you are put!' he declared. 'There ain't no sense of you tryin' to get away, anyhow!' he added. 'The chief don't mean to let you go anywhere until he's had a chanst to palaver. You was a damn fool to ride over here, anyway!'

He went out, locking the door behind him. An hour later she saw him pass one of the windows, and she called to him, asking him to come in and loosen the ropes which bound her hands together, for her hands were numb and her arms aching.

Naylor entered, looked at the rope.

'I reckon you ain't got a hell of a chanst to get away, anyhow,' he decided. 'You ain't got no hoss, an' walkin' ain't no picnic. Besides, I'll be hangin' around.'

He removed the rope and moved to the door, where he stood and watched her as she got up from the chair and rubbed her wrists to restore circulation. Then she faced him.

'Naylor,' she said, 'if you will let me go I promise to say nothing about your being concerned with what has happened to Watt Hamlin and the Porters. I will even swear that you were helping me all the time!'

'That's no good,' Naylor replied. He smiled crookedly. 'There ain't no chanst to you gettin' away. Travis was sendin' some of the boys south to watch all the trails in case I didn't ketch you. You'll never get to where you can do any talkin'! I reckon you don't know Travis. You'll be sorry you rode over this way. An' whatever he does to you, nobody will interfere!'

He went outside and locked the door.

Edna stood for a time thinking of Naylor's words. Their suggestion of impending evil had filled her with dismay, but it had been the man's manner which had really convinced her of the hopelessness of trying to escape.

Naylor was impressed with a sense of Travis's omnipotence. It was evident that he felt that when once Travis decided, there was absolutely no use in attempting to fight back. One might as well surrender with what grace one could.

As she stood in the room of the cabin now, her thoughts went to last night, when she had seen him sitting on the edge of the table which was at that instant close to her. A great fear of him welled up in her, shortening her breath, bringing a queer constriction into her throat, and in that instant she decided she would rather die by Naylor's gun than be imprisoned in the cabin to wait until Travis came. She wouldn't face him!

One of the windows of the room in which she stood was open. While watching Naylor she had discovered that at frequent intervals he passed the window. Often he stood just in front of it for a few minutes, shading his hands as he peered westward. She felt that Naylor was momentarily expecting Travis to appear. Naylor was impatient. Two or three times she had heard him curse.

Edna went to a cast-iron stove that stood in a corner of the room and took up the short, heavy iron poker she found there. Then she stole to the wall near the window and waited.

Twice as she stood beside the window with the poker upraised, Naylor passed just beyond reach of the implement. But the third time he passed he came close to the window, and Edna leaned out and struck with all her force.

She felt that she had not struck accurately, for her weapon glanced from Naylor's head and struck one of his shoulders. The poker flew out of her grasp, but she saw Naylor go down, and she was certain she had stunned him. Climbing through the window, she dropped beside him, intending to run to his horse, mount it, and do her best to reach the

Circle Dot in spite of the riders Travis had thrown out to intercept her.

She stepped over Naylor. As she did so, one of his hands flashed out and grasped her right ankle, throwing her off balance. She fell upon an arm and shoulder, kicked herself free, and scrambled to her feet as Naylor rose and threw himself at her. Naylor slipped as he lunged, for his shoulder struck her in the back, throwing her headlong against the wall of the cabin.

There was a terrific roaring in her ears. A vast darkness, strangely dotted with little splotches of light, seemed to surround her. Then came an interval in which she heard nothing, saw nothing.

## CHAPTER FIFTEEN

It seemed to Edna that she was floating upward out of a black pit when she again discerned the little splotches of light. The roaring in her ears had diminished, although there had been one crash which still seemed to reverberate like a great gun being fired at a distance. She could not definitely fix the time when the great gun had boomed; she was in doubt as to whether it had sounded before the splotches of light appeared, or afterward.

When she opened her eyes to see daylight

around her, she was still trying to determine the moment of the crash, and not for several seconds did she become aware that a man's face was in her vision, and that the man's face was Nevins's.

She was lying comfortably; she felt a pillow under her head. And after a time she realized that Nevins was sitting on a chair close to her, intently and reassuringly watching her.

Her first emotion was one of astonishment.

'How on earth did you get here?' she asked. 'I am still in the cabin, I suppose?'

He answered the last question first.

'Yes, you are still here,' he said. 'I just happened along, an' saw Naylor divin' at you.'

She sat erect, gazing dizzily around.

'Where is Naylor now?' she asked.

'He's where he won't devil a woman again.'

'Dead?'

He nodded.

She cringed, horrified, and watched him through a silence. At last, feeling that she needed to explain her presence at the cabin, she told him why she had come, and that on her way back from Willets Naylor had seized her.

'I reckoned it was somethin' like that,' he remarked. 'I saw your wrists.' He was watching her narrowly, and she thought that in his eyes she could detect a gleam of admiration.

'So you saw Travis,' he said. 'An' did he offer to help you?'

'Help me!'

He smiled without mirth at the scorn in her voice. She told him of her talk with Travis, and related what she had overheard between Travis and Naylor. After the entire story had been told, she was astonished that Nevins showed no surprise.

'You knew Travis?' she asked. 'You knew he was behind those murders?'

'No,' he said. 'But I ain't surprised. I'd sized Travis up as bein' that kind of a man.' She observed a troubled light come into his eyes. 'You shouldn't have interfered,' he said. 'You shouldn't have come here. It was a mighty brave thing to do, but foolish. A woman has no business ridin' around this country alone.'

'I would do it again, in the same circumstances,' she declared. 'I could not let Nellie Porter go with Adams without offering some objection!'

'No,' he conceded, the odd glint again in his eyes, 'you couldn't.' He smiled. 'But it can't be helped now. You've forced Travis to show his hand, an' now we've got to fight him in the open.' For an instant a fire smouldered in his eyes and then died out, an ironic gleam remaining.

'If Travis has thrown his men out, as he told Naylor, we ain't in shape to do a terrible lot of fightin'. Travis has about fifty men at his beck an' call, if we count those that have been suspected of crooked deals. I reckon right now Travis has thrown a ring around this section, to keep you from gettin' away.'

'But you got through,' she said hopefully.

'I've been through,' he answered. 'I've been two days gettin' this far from the Circle Dot. Last night an' the day before I was restin', not feelin' very much like ridin'. I wasn't half a mile from here. But I was headed for here, knowin' the place.

'This is the old Rignal ranch,' he went on. 'The Rignals lived here until they died. The house hasn't been used until now, though it looks like Travis an' his gang have been here a lot. While you was unconscious I was lookin' around. There's a big stock of supplies, grub an' such. They must have stayed here often.'

He drew out his heavy revolver, stuck it between his knees, opened the cylinder, and with his right hand drew out two smoke-blackened empty cartridges. Then, still using his right hand, he drew two fresh cartridges from the belt around his waist, inserted them into the chambers he had emptied, snapped the cylinder back into place and replaced the weapon in its holster.

He had made no attempt to use his left hand; during the process of unloading and reloading the revolver the left hand had hung limply at his side.

With an inward gasp, Edna remembered that his left arm had been injured in the fight with Logan, the deputy. She stiffened as she looked at his hand. It was swollen badly and inflamed. The fingers were puffed and stiff. She knew what had happened. Fever had set in; the arm and hand were infected. For an instant, as a chill of apprehension stole over her, she sat nerveless and bewildered.

And in that instant she realized that upon awakening and seeing him sitting near her, she had depended upon him to extricate her from the danger that threatened her. Now she knew that if Nevins's condition grew worse her chances of escape would be lessened.

She got up quickly, took a tin basin from the kitchen, went outside and filled the basin with water, tore a piece of cloth from an undergarment, and reentered the room where Nevins still sat, his chin on his chest.

He said nothing as she ripped the sleeve of his shirt open and folded it back into the armhole of his vest. She grew very white as the arm was disclosed to her sight, for it was much puffed, and great, angry-looking streaks ran for a considerable distance from a wound in the forearm.

Logan's bullet had gone clear through the arm at a point several inches from the elbow, or about midway between the elbow and the wrist. The wound was through the big muscle, and she felt it had missed the bone. Nevins must have lost much blood, although the wound would not have been dangerous had it received proper treatment.

Later, when she had finished bandaging the arm, he stood erect and looked at her. His face was unnaturally flushed.

'Thank you,' he said; 'that feels a lot better. But if this place is what you say it is, we'd better be makin' tracks out of here. You don't want to be around here when Travis an' his gang get here.'

He stood, reeling just a little as he gazed at some shelves on the kitchen wall.

'There's grub,' he said. 'You'll be needin' it. You'll have to hide out for a few days. I know a place where nobody will find you. You can't go back to the Circle Dot. Fagin's there, an' Fagin ain't to be trusted. An' there'll be others there. You'd never get to Deming.'

He pointed to a gunny-sack lying on the floor in a corner of the kitchen. 'We'll fill that with grub,' he added. 'Then I'll take you to that place I was tellin' you about. After you're settled, I'll come back here an' lay for Travis an' his bunch. An' after I've settled them I'll ride to Fort Bayard an' have a talk with that major. I'm not trustin' Callahan, after him sending that deputy after me.'

Not waiting for her to reply, he got the gunny-sack, instructed her to hold it, and filled it with various articles of food from the shelves.

He tied the bag with a short rope which he found on the floor—the rope that had been around Edna's wrists; then he swung the bag under his right arm and carried it outside. Edna followed him, observing with dismay that he staggered a little.

She mounted Naylor's horse, then turned her head and watched him as he swung into the saddle. She saw him wince as he swung up, but once he settled back against the cantle he smiled.

'Now you wouldn't think that a man would need two arms to do his ridin'. But he gets used to usin' both, an' when one is gone he misses it.'

Saying nothing more, he urged his horse northward, over the trail which had brought Edna to the cabin the night before.

They came, after a while, to a little level high among some ragged, towering peaks. Southward, shutting from view the lower country from which they had come, was a wall of granite perhaps a hundred feet higher than the level on which they stood. To the right and left of the granite wall ran miniature cañons, corridors with rocks walls and roofs, caves.

In front of them, to the north, beginning at the bottom of a slope not more than a dozen feet below them, was a vast green level. It stretched for several miles to the hills that rimmed it, northward; east and west it merged into other hills.

Near the center of the level ran a narrow stream of water, white and sparkling in the sun. Near by were trees that spread an inviting shade.

'Oh!' exclaimed Edna, as the two halted their horses and sat motionless, mentally absorbing the beauty of the picture, 'isn't it wonderful! How in the world did you happen to discover this place?'

'I reckon I'm the only one that knows about it,' he replied. 'Except for Svenson, an old sheep rancher and hermit who lived here. But Svenson's dead now.'

Edna repeated what she had told him of the conversation between Naylor and Travis, when he had said: 'An' Matt thinkin' he was hangin' Ross Nevins! But anyhow, Matt got Hamlin.' Edna added that if he could reach the sheriff he could clear himself.

'Yes,' he said, 'I've thought of that. It's mighty plain the whole thing was a frame-up, Indians an' all. I'll get to Callahan. But you've got to stay here until I do.'

He looked long at her, and it appeared to her that he was having some difficulty in finding her. The light in his eyes had dulled, his face was a ghastly white, and he was holding tightly to the pommel of the saddle. Apparently having succeeded in getting her into his vision, he smiled.

'I'll be showin' you the place where you'll have to live until I get back,' he said. 'It's right over here.'

He wheeled his horse and sent it along the edge of the level, westward.

Edna followed him, and observed with dismay that he swayed perilously, and that his head kept drooping forward, jerkily, in the manner of a man sitting erect in a chair, napping, and trying to fight off drowsiness.

He rode onward, though, until after passing through a narrow passageway hewn in the solid rock he reached another level. Here he halted and waved his right arm.

'Svenson's house,' he announced.

Amazed, Edna stared. They were on a circular level, not more than fifty feet in diameter. The rock wall, which on the level they had just left had towered about a hundred feet above them, had sloped downward until it was not more than thirty or forty feet high. But above their heads was a giant overhang that arched out over them like a huge, inverted bowl.

The arch formed a great cave, with smooth, painted walls. Along its edge grew ferns whose long fronds drooped until she could almost touch them. In the rear of the cave, against the smooth wall, was a rock ledge several feet wide and perhaps eight or ten feet above the level upon which their horses stood. Edna rose close to it, and although she rose in the stirrups she could not see over its edge.

There was a balcony of logs around the edge of the ledge, and a ladder leaning against it. The ladder was light, and Edna felt that it had purposely been made that way to facilitate drawing it upward to the ledge. She was certain that her conclusion was correct when she observed a bunk on the ledge.

She finished her inspection of the ledge, and her attention was attracted to the east wall of the cave, where wood-ashes and charred sticks showed where Svenson had built his fires. And she saw that the narrow passageway through which they had entered had a door, or a heavy gate built of slender saplings lashed together with leathery vines, the gate itself swinging from heavy pegs driven into crevices of the wall. There was a heavy bar, and slots into which the bar could be slid.

The passageway formed the only means of entrance or egress. Once in this place, Svenson had no need to worry about wild animals that might be prowling about. And that, Edna now realized, had been his chief concern when Nevins had proposed coming here.

But at this moment Edna's thoughts went to Nevins.

He was unlashing the bag of provisions

155

they had brought from the Rignal cabin, and as she watched him the bag fell to the floor of the cave. Nevins sat, leaning over a little, gazing down at it. Then he straightened and looked straight at Edna.

'I reckon that's all, Svenson,' he said. 'Nobody will bother you here—you or your sheep. I'll be headin' back this way after I've killed Travis!'

He wheeled his horse and sent it into the narrow passageway. He vanished, swaying from side to side.

With a cry Edna rode after him, and she was not yet through the passageway when she saw him. His horse had halted on the little level from which they had viewed the valley. The animal was standing motionless, the reins dragging. Close to him, lying on his right side on the smooth stone of the level, was Nevins.

Nevins was unconscious. She knelt beside him and felt his pulse. It was weak, and he was breathing heavily.

She arose and stood for an instant looking down at him; and while she was wondering what she ought to do for him, she was aware that she was also speculating over the physical frailty that had brought him down. A man of his apparent ruggedness should not so quickly succumb to a wound which, although painful, had not touched a vital spot.

She got on her horse and rode back through the passageway to the cave, where in a corner on a shelf of rock she had seen a wooden pail in which was some water covered with a greenish slime. With the pail dangling from her hand she rode down the slope into the valley until she reached the stream of water she had seen from the first level.

Kneeling on the grassy bank of the stream, she scrubbed the inside of the pail with sand and water until it was as clean as she could make it. Then she filled it with the clear, sparkling water of the stream, mounted the horse, and rode back to Nevins.

He had not moved. She opened his mouth and let some water from a cupped hand drop between his lips. Then with another cloth torn from her garments she bathed his head and neck. Once when the water partly revived him he opened his eyes and looked at her as though puzzled.

Resolutely she unbuttoned his shirt, working it off his arms and down over his shoulders. But before she got the garment off, her face had blanched and her eyes had grown wide with dismay.

For the wound in his arm was not the only one he had received. Low down on his left side, just above the hip, was another. He had not spoken about it, through fear of worrying her, she supposed. But this was the wound which had weakened him, and which had finally brought him down.

For the first time since she had set out

upon the journey which had taken her to Judge Travis she was shaken. She got to her feet and stood facing the emerald valley into which Nevins had brought her. She did not speak, but in her thoughts was a plea, repeated many times:

'God help me to save him!'

## CHAPTER SIXTEEN

Getting Nevins out of the sunshine of the open level into the shady coolness of the cave was a task that required all of Edna's strength and courage and patience. Yet she had no intention of giving Nevins up, no thought of deserting him. She was grimly determined not to let him die.

She ran back to the outside level and got another pail of water from the stream. Then, almost denuding herself of her skirt, she soaked pieces of cloth in the cool water and laid them on the wounds. Frequently she forced water through Nevins's lips.

Her thoughts ran to tales of animals healing wounds by means of mud wallows, and she went again to the stream, where she observed a thick stratum of adobe mud. She might apply that. But there was danger that the mud might create new infection or supplement the old, and she went back to

Nevins empty-handed. She had heard of sheep tallow as being a remedy.

Later, having nerved herself to the ordeal of killing a sheep, she got Nevins into a comfortable position, bathed the wounds again, and laid freshly wet clothes upon them, gave him a final drink of water, and went out again to the level, where she took Nevins's rifle from its saddle-sheath and secured a knife.

Then she mounted her horse and rode down into the valley. Dusk was beginning to settle when she returned. She was pale and shaking, but resolute. She had killed a sheep.

She found Nevins as he had been when she left him, and apparently his condition had not changed.

Out on the level she found some small sticks of dried mesquite, and she obtained matches from a pocket of Nevins's vest. Soon she had a fire going, and she discovered a small pan in the corner where she had found the pail.

Half an hour later she again bathed Nevins's wounds, then dried them and applied the tallow she had procured.

All that night and the next day she stayed awake watching Nevins, bathing his forehead, moistening his fevered lips with cool water.

Late in the afternoon of the third day she climbed to the bunk on the rock ledge and slept. When she awoke, dusk had come again, and she descended the ladder and knelt beside Nevins.

Laying a hand on his forehead, she found it almost as cool as her own. The coolness frightened her and she shrank back with a gasp, for she was afraid that death had come upon him while she had slept. But at her startled movement he opened his eyes. His gaze, quiet and sane, met hers. Then he glanced upward and for a space seemed to speculate upon his surroundings. At last he looked at her again and smiled.

'I'm still here,' he said. 'I thought I'd been ridin', an' I kept wonderin' how it was you was around all the time. I thought I'd left you, to go an' look for Travis. I've been here all the time, I reckon?'

'Yes,' she whispered, answering his smile. 'For three days.'

★    ★    ★

The days were long after Nevins's return to consciousness but to Edna they were not monotonous. She cared little whether she ever left the valley. And she observed, with a vague feeling which was almost regret, that Nevins grew stronger daily.

The stronger he grew, the less he depended upon her, the more indifferent he became to her presence. There were times when she could see gratitude glowing in his eyes, but nothing more. Not the expression she wanted to see in them.

She tried not to permit him to see what had happened to her, although there were times, when she was close to him or when she approached him to dress his wounds, that she blushed furiously. She was aware of the blushes, for at those times he could feel her cheeks burning. He evidently did not see them.

As a matter of fact, Nevins seldom looked at her unless she spoke to him. As the days passed he became able to walk about, and often when she entered the cave to look for him he was outside in the valley.

They had been occupying the cave for about ten days when, as they were sitting on the edge of the level above the green slope that led down into the valley, he looked straight at her, his gaze probing.

'Svenson must have enjoyed this place,' he said.

'He couldn't help it,' she agreed.

'Meanin' that you have enjoyed it?' he went on, his voice slightly incredulous.

'Very much.'

'H'm. Not much here for a girl that has been used to havin' comforts.'

'Sometimes one gets along very well without the things the world calls comforts.'

'Depends upon the point of view,' he said

161

evenly. 'We can get accustomed to a great many things when we have to. No use to complain. Complainin' won't make things different. That's it, ain't it?'

She couldn't tell him that she would be content to stay here for the remainder of her natural life, providing he stayed with her. She was compelled to answer in the affirmative.

He laughed softly.

'You are something of a philosopher, after all,' he remarked. 'The first time I saw you I thought different.'

'Just what did you think?'

'You wantin' the truth?' he asked.

'Certainly.'

'I thought you was mighty proud. Stuck up, as they say out here. I don't mind tellin' you that you have surprised me.'

'How?'

'By the way you have acted since I tumbled over. By the way you have adjusted yourself to this condition. Most girls would have fizzled out. You took right hold as though you'd lived in a place like this all your life. All of which pretty near convinces me that there's a heap of virtue in pride. It seems to hold its head up in adversity.'

'It isn't pride,' she denied; 'it is fear. I stayed here with you because I was afraid Travis would catch me.'

'Well,' he said, 'it's a mighty good thing for me that you got afraid of Travis. It seems to me I had a narrow squeak. I was pretty far gone when I fell off my horse about here. I'm thankin' you for stickin' to me.'

His voice had been low and inexpressive. In the same tone and with the same lack of emphasis or fervor he might have thanked her for watching his horse for a few minutes. It was the first time he had mentioned her service to him, and she had been expecting the thanks to come. And now it was over, and he had been as indifferent about it as about everything.

She turned her head away, for even though the dusk had come she was afraid he would see the pain in her eyes. If there had only been a ring of sincerity in his voice! But there hadn't been.

She was certain he had thanked her merely for the sake of being polite to her. He hadn't really appreciated her service, and she was positive that behind his indifference were cynicism and mockery. He hadn't observed the change in her; he still saw her as she had been when she had alighted from the train at Deming.

How could she make him understand that she was not the girl she had been at Deming and during the few days immediately following? How could she make him feel that the events and experiences of the last few weeks had transformed her, had given her a new viewpoint of life, had brought her a clearer understanding of the basic values of manhood and womanhood? What a fool she had been in those days!—days that now seemed remote, as if belonging to a previous existence!

She knew it was shameful of her to confess, even to herself, that she was ready to throw herself into his arms if he would accept her. And yet she felt no shame. She had lost all her pride and her arrogance.

'No thanks are necessary,' she said, answering him. 'I was glad to be able to partly repay you.'

'Repay me for what?'

'For your attitude in the question of partnership in the Circle Dot.' She paused. 'And for your generosity,' she added.

'Repay me for bein' honest?' He laughed. 'That's the first time I ever heard of honesty bein' called generosity. What you had comin' belonged to you. I had no right to hang on to any part of it. You don't owe me anything for that. Besides, maybe I had another idea than just honesty. Maybe I was wantin' to show you that I wasn't the sort of man you'd been hatin' so hard.'

'Are you sure I did hate you?' she asked. 'Perhaps I was merely offended at your treatment of me.'

She didn't know at this minute whether she wanted to slap him or burst out crying. She felt like doing both, because of the quiet, mocking laughter in his voice. She was very serious, and she felt that he had no right to sit there and calmly refuse to understand that she was trying to apologize.

She had, metaphorically, gone headlong against the wall of his indifference, and she was dazed and chagrined because she had made no impression upon it. Moreover, she was convinced that she now hated him more than ever, and she certainly would never again make any tentative advances. He was too completely absorbed in himself, she decided as she sat there in the dusk studying his profile; he was too satisfied with himself, too much of an egotist to understand or realize that persons other than himself had capacity for feeling.

But, watching him, she doubted that conclusion. He was aware that others could feel, for at times she had observed his eyes glow with keen perception and subtle knowledge and understanding, even sympathy. But toward her, particularly, he had steeled himself. He was showing her that he didn't care for her.

The silence between them lasted long. Apparently he was in no mood to talk, and she was determined she would never speak to him again.

# CHAPTER SEVENTEEN

After Edna had ridden westward into the dimly luminous stretch of country that lay between the Circle Dot and Willets, Grace Rignal stole back into the house.

She was awake with the dawn, and shortly she was downstairs working in the kitchen. She was so excited that she herself had no appetite, but she knew Fagin would want breakfast, and that she must make a pretence of surprise when Fagin, discovering Edna's absence, asked questions.

Half an hour after she reached the kitchen she heard him come downstairs. She pretended not to see him, and he spoke:

'You're up early. I reckon you knowed your new boss would be hungry.'

She turned then to see him grinning at her, widely, confidently.

'I'm getting breakfast as usual,' she retorted. 'If you are near when it is served, you may have yours. I certainly shall not call you.'

'Sort of on the peck this mornin', eh?' he said. His grin vanished and became a malicious smirk. 'I'm one of the kind of boarders that's always around at meal time,' he added. 'Don't call me if it's goin' to strain your voice.'

He walked away from the doorway. Grace could hear him cross the living room, the porch. For half an hour she heard no sound from him, and then he suddenly stuck his head in the kitchen doorway. His eyes were cold and probing.

'Where's that Pendleton girl?' he asked.

'Why,' said Grace, with a good pretence of casualness, 'she is somewhere around, I suppose. She came downstairs with me, and I presume she is walking about somewhere.'

Fagin was watching her intently.

'She ain't around somewhere,' he announced, 'an' there's a hoss gone.'

'I suppose that indicates she has gone riding,' calmly said Grace. 'But she said nothing to me about going.'

Fagin stepped into the kitchen. He stood over Grace as she worked at the stove.

'I reckon you knowed that when I took charge here I intended no one was to leave here without me sayin' so?'

'That's the first I've heard of such an order,' said Grace. 'At any rate, I'm here. If you care to repeat your order to Miss Pendleton you will have to find her.'

'No damn foolin' goes!' declared Fagin. His voice had suddenly become hoarse with passion. He gripped Grace by the arms, dragged her away from the stove and drew her close to him, holding her arms so tightly that a cry of pain was forced from her.

'No damn foolin'!' he declared again. 'You tell me where that Pendleton girl has gone or I'll choke hell out of you!'

Fagin slipped his hands to her throat, which was still sore and swollen from Adams's attack the day before. The light in Fagin's eyes was not so frenzied as that which had been in Adams's, but it was fully as intense and malignant.

'Don't, Fagin!' she gasped. 'I'll tell you.'

'Thought you knowed!' he said exultantly. His fingers worked at her neck and her flesh cringed under them.

'Spit it out!' he ordered.

'She has gone to see Judge Travis!' Grace told him. 'She doesn't believe Judge Travis gave his consent to what you and Adams are trying to do. She doesn't believe Adams had any right to take Nellie Porter away from here!'

She had expected Fagin to exhibit rage at this news, and she was prepared to feel the grip of his fingers again upon her throat. To her vast astonishment he released her, dropped into a chair, and laughed.

'By God!' he finally ejaculated, 'that's good! That's a humdinger! Haw, haw, haw! Why, that saves the judge a ride over here! He was comin' this mornin' to see the Pendleton girl! He saw her in Deming an' took a shine to her! An' she's run right over to his place!'

He suddenly sobered and looked at her with a speculative gaze.

'Now ain't women damn fools!' he ejaculated. 'Here's me, which wouldn't hurt her. I ain't good enough to be around. But she'll drag it over to Willets an' go to beggin' Travis for God's sake to take Fagin away from the Circle Dot!'

'Travis is a judge,' responded Grace. 'Moreover, he is a gentleman!'

Fagin grinned satirically.

'He's which?' he said. A huge mirth swelled his cheeks, and he placed a hand over his lips, seemingly in an effort to keep Grace from discovering the amusement he felt. 'Yes,' he added, deliberately winking, 'the judge is a gentleman. Make no mistake about that!'

Grace got away from Fagin as soon as she could. She spent most of the day in her room, anxiously awaiting Edna's return. And as dusk began to fall and Edna did not appear, she began to meditate upon Fagin's strange manner when Travis's name had been mentioned.

She didn't see Fagin around, and so when the dusk came she went downstairs and began to prepare supper. After a while she went out upon the front porch for a breath of air, and saw Edna's horse standing at the porch edge.

Riderless the animal stood, its head drooping, its sides and muzzle splotched and

169

ruffled from dried perspiration. It breathed wheezily and heavily.

Grace looked long at the horse and a divination of tragedy seized her. Her lips grew white and she backed against the jambs of the front door, breathing fast, her brain whirling.

While she stood there, dismayed and undecided, she saw Fagin coming toward her from the stable.

She watched Fagin, remembering what he had said about Travis, and she perceived from the light that leaped into his eyes that he was not surprised at sight of the riderless horse.

He walked close to the animal and judicially examined it, although Grace was aware that he was furtively watching her also.

'Winded,' he drawled. 'He's run some.' He listened, turning his head to one side. 'Foundered,' he added. 'Might as well feed him to the coyotes.' He now looked full at Grace.

'Where did he come from?' he asked. 'Seems I seen that hoss here, in the corral, didn't I?'

'That is a Circle Dot horse,' said Grace. 'You don't mean to say you didn't see the brand!'

'Why, shucks! So it is!' He now looked searchingly at Grace. 'I've been wonderin' if that ain't the hoss the Pendleton girl rode this mornin'?'

When Grace did not answer him he grinned widely.

'Hit it first pop!' he said. 'Well, it looks like she must have seen Travis, eh?'

Grace ran through the living room and up the stairs to her own room, where she threw herself on the bed. She told herself that she didn't believe that Edna had met Travis. She couldn't believe that Travis was the kind of man Fagin had hinted at so vividly in his ill-considered speech of the morning. Fagin had been merely trying to frighten her.

And yet something must have happened to Edna. She knew horses, and she was aware that the riderless animal had been ridden mercilessly to get into that condition, and she felt Edna would not have ridden him like that unless some terrible danger had threatened her.

Perhaps she had not even reached Willets!

Grace got up from the bed and began to put on her riding garments. Her eyes were alight with determination. She herself would ride to Willets. If Edna hadn't reached there, she would ride to Deming to seek help from Sheriff Callahan.

She knew, though, that Fagin would not permit her to leave the house. So instead of descending to the first floor by the stairs, she entered Nevins's room, swung herself over the window-sill and dropped to the shed roof.

171

She made the short leap from the shed roof to the ground noiselessly, landing on her toes and permitting herself to pitch forward upon her outstretched hands. She stood for an instant where she had landed, listening.

She went through the darkness until she reached the stable door. She was just about to pass through the big opening when she heard a voice so close to her that she felt if she had taken half a dozen additional steps she would have collided with its owner.

'So Travis didn't get her?'

The voice belonged to Fagin. There was slight mockery in it.

'He didn't,' said another voice, which Grace did not recognize. 'Some way, she gave him the slip. An' he was after her, hell bent! She'd been to see him at Willets. He was smooth with her, like he always is. Somehow, he got her sore an' she talked.

'Travis an' Naylor was in the Rignal shack last night, talkin' over things. Seems the Pendleton girl was at a window listenin'. She told Travis things him an' Naylor had said. Travis was sure wild. Him an' Naylor had busted loose with everything they knowed.

'They was talkin' about how they'd set them Indians on Nevins an' Seaton an' the Pendleton girl when they was ridin' to the Circle Dot from Deming, an' they was gassin' about how they'd set the Indians on the Porter place; how Matt Blandell had knifed

172

Hamlin an' had tried to hang Seaton, thinkin' Seaton was Nevins. The Pendleton girl heard the whole lot of it.'

'Hell's fire!' cursed Fagin. 'Damn her! We'll have them soldiers over to Fort Bayard after us if that girl goes to blabbin'!'

'That's what's eatin' Travis,' said the strange voice. 'Gentlemen, be calm! Travis has gone plumb loco! He's ragin'! He sent Naylor after the Pendleton girl soon as she rode out of Willets. He told Naylor if he didn't ketch the girl he'd tear him apart!

'Well, Naylor ain't worryin' about that right now. Right after noon the chief an' half a dozen of the boys rode to the Rignal shack, where Naylor was to bring the girl an' wait there for Travis. Naylor was there, right enough, but the girl wasn't. Naylor was layin' sort of humped up on the ground just under a winder. He'd been bored through the back of the head, an' the girl was gone. The chief kicked Naylor. That red hair of his was standin' straight up!

'The girl had been there. There were pieces of cloth from a skirt layin' around. There was a pan of water somebody had been soakin' some blood off of somebody with. Looked like it.

'There was no blood on Naylor exceptin' on his head, an' that hadn't been touched. An' the chief had give Naylor orders not to hurt the girl. Besides, there was tracks where

173

a strange hoss had come out of that box cañon behind the shack. An' we found a place in the cañon where a man had camped. Somebody had took the grub we had cached in the shack. Looks like some man must have run into Naylor an' the girl. He plugged Naylor an' lit out with the girl.

'The chief has got a dozen of the boys combin' the country between the shack an' Deming. There's another dozen scourin' things clean north. They're runnin' around in circles, for the chief swears that if we don't bring that girl in he'll clean up the whole gang an' light out of the country!

'Far as that goes, we'll all have to pull our freight if the soldiers get to hearin' what's happened, an' who's been behind what's goin' on. The chief sorta dropped a hint that he wouldn't care a hell of a lot if the Pendleton girl didn't show up any more, anywhere.' There was a pause. 'So you ain't seen her?' he added.

'Her hoss came back here. He'd been winded.'

'Naylor chased her, I reckon. We found a place in that gully near the Saw-tooth where somebody's hoss had backed. We figger that's where Naylor throwed his rope when he ketched her.'

'Where's the other boys that are with you?' asked Fagin.

'Waitin' back a piece. I didn't want them to
174

bust in before I knowed what was goin' on here. Figgered that mebbe the Circle Dot outfit was in.'

His voice changed, became freighted with a note of warning.

'You step light an' easy when the chief sees you, Fagin. He's blamin' you for lettin' the Pendleton girl get away from here. Swears if you ain't got a good explanation he'll bust you wide open!'

Fagin did not answer. There followed another silence, and then the stranger spoke.

'Well, I reckon I'll be hittin' it back.' Again there fell a silence, and again the man spoke. 'You heard anything about Ross Nevins? Adams said he drilled Logan an' lit out. The chief was thinkin' mebbe the guy which done Naylor in was Nevins. An' the chief ain't strong for brushin' agin Nevins. He sorta paled when he was talkin' about him.'

'Nevins ain't been heard from. But mebbe it was him that downed Naylor. You can't never tell anything about Nevins.'

'Well, so long.'

Grace heard the man walking away. She stood, breathing fast, waiting, listening. She waited so long that it appeared to her Fagin had gone too, and she was on the point of moving toward the stable door when she heard Fagin's voice, seemingly coming from the spot where she had heard it before.

'Hell's fire!' he exclaimed.

Fagin moved—toward her! Before she could force her muscles to answer the command her brain flashed to them, he lurched against her. He started, cursed, and his arms came out, encircling her.

She fought him frenziedly, unavailingly. For with little effort he swept her from her feet, gripping her so hard that her breath left her, holding her so tightly to him that she could not reach his face with her hands. Thus he carried her to the house, across the porch and into the living room, where a light shone from a lamp on a center table.

He set her down, held her at arm's length and grinned at her, his teeth bared with the malignance of an animal about to attack. His face was pale, he was breathing fast, and when he spoke his voice was dry and light.

'You damn sneak! You heard Ed Talfer talkin' to me! You stood there takin' it all in! You heard every word he said, for when Ed first come there I seemed to hear a step, but thought I was mistaken. You'll be sorry you didn't mind your own business, for you know too much to be let travel around loose!'

She was thoroughly frightened at Fagin's manner, but she resolutely faced him.

'So that is how Judge Travis administers the law!' she said. 'That is why you were appointed to look after the Circle Dot. Oh, I wish Bob Nevins had known that!'

Fagin's lips smirked in feline mirth.

'You got to admit it was a smart scheme,' he said. 'An' nobody would have got next to it if it wasn't for you women nosin' around. But Travis will get the Pendleton woman, an' he'll fix her so's she won't go around blabbin'. An' you won't do no blabbin', either!'

He was still gripping her shoulders, and now when she observed his eyes widen she divined he was on the verge of muscular action, violence. The light in his eyes had grown sinister with evil purpose. She felt he was thinking of Judge Travis's threat, communicated to him by the man Ed Talfer!

She relaxed her body as though shrinking from him, and he chuckled mockingly. The next instant a curse came from him, for Grace had suddenly torn herself free and was running to a corner of the room.

Fagin lunged after her. But her movement had been swift and unexpected, and before Fagin had taken half a dozen steps down the long room Grace was facing him again, looking at him with blazing eyes from behind the muzzle of a rifle.

The weapon had reposed in the corner since the evening of the previous day, when Brandt Adams had wrested it from her grasp, unloaded it, and flung it to the ground at the edge of the porch.

After Adams had gone and Fagin had temporarily absented himself, Grace had picked up the rifle, reloaded it, and stood it in the corner. Now the weapon was steady in her hands, and a finger trembled on the trigger.

Fagin snarled, but halted.

'Put that gun down!' he ordered.

'No,' she answered. 'You are going to leave the Circle Dot. I am going to give you ten seconds. If you are not outside that door in that time, I am going to kill you!'

Fagin bared his teeth. He leaped sideways, and at the same instant dropped his right hand to the butt of the heavy revolver at his right hip.

The rifle crashed spitefully. A lance of flame and smoke leaped at Fagin, struck his right arm near the shoulder. He yelled with pain and staggered back to the doorway, where he stood, his face working with hate and baffled fury.

There was no word spoken. But Fagin saw no mercy in the eyes that still blazed at him from behind the muzzle of the rifle, and he wheeled and plunged out of the doorway into the darkness.

The instant Fagin vanished Grace sprang to the lamp and blew out the flame. Then she darted to a doorway and ran upstairs to her room. Reaching the door, she stood in it for some seconds, listening to the crashes which told her that Fagin, standing outside, was shooting into the living room. She had expected that of him!

Fagin would kill her if he got the opportunity. She had seen murder in his eyes when she had faced him.

She stood for some minutes in the doorway of her room, panting and excited. She knew Fagin would not cease his efforts to kill her. Travis would hold him accountable for her, and he meant to kill her to keep her from telling what she had overheard.

She entered her room, locked the door, and drew up the window-shade. Then she placed a chair in a corner where she could see the door and the window and at the same time be out of range should Fagin shoot through either.

But although she sat there until the dawn came, she heard no sound from Fagin. She dared not sleep, dared not open the door of her room, lest Fagin be lurking in the hallway ready to pounce upon her. Later in the morning she heard him walking downstairs, and after a while an odor of cooking penetrated her room.

About mid-morning she heard Fagin go out. But she did not open the door, fearing a trick. It was not until, watching from her window, she saw Fagin walking across the level that stretched between the house and the stable that she even considered opening the door. She was afraid one of Fagin's friends might have joined him during the night.

She wasn't hungry, and she drank water from a pitcher on the stand in her room. She knew that Fagin could not get at her except through the door or the window. He could not break the door down without her hearing him, nor could he place a ladder against the wall under the window without making some sound that would warn her.

And so shortly after midday she stretched out on the bed, facing the window, with her rifle lying beside her. She had plenty of cartridges.

Toward evening she heard Fagin come into the house again. For a while she heard him walking back and forth downstairs, and after a while came the clumping of his boots up the stairs and into the hallway.

He halted in the hall near the door of her room, and she felt that from the sound of his voice he was not standing directly in front of the door, but to one side of it, where he would be out of range should she shoot through the door.

'Look here,' he said gruffly, 'I want to talk to you!'

'Go ahead,' suggested Grace.

'I ain't goin' to talk through no damn door!' he declared.

'Nobody asked you to! And if you touch that door I shall shoot through it!'

'What you sayin'?' he demanded. 'I can't hear you.'

Grace laughed.

'That's too crude, Fagin!' she jeered. 'I know you intend to kill me, if you can, and I am not going to stand in front of the door and give you a chance.'

'Wise, eh?' he growled. 'Well, I'll get you before long. But if you come out here an' promise not to tell anybody what you heard me an' Ed Talfer talkin' about, I'll just tie you up for a few days an' not hurt you.'

'Thanks,' she responded scornfully. 'I would much rather stay where I am.'

'You'll get damn hungry before you get out of there!' he asserted. 'Gadd an' Seaton can't get back here inside of five or six days.'

Grace did not answer.

There followed a silence, during which she could hear Fagin muttering to himself, although she could not distinguish his words. Then she heard him walking down the hallway to the stairs.

He went down, crossed the porch. Half an hour later, while Grace still reclined on the bed listening, a bullet whined through the open window and thudded against a beam of the ceiling of her room.

From the nature of the report, Grace knew Fagin was using a rifle. But unless he could find some eminence from which he could direct his bullets so that they would come horizontally, there was little danger that one of them would strike her.

The bed on which she lay was some distance from the window, and several feet to the right of it, as she faced it. And she knew there was no building to the left from which Fagin might send his bullets.

She was frightened, though, and lay perfectly still while Fagin shot again and again. Splinters from the ceiling beams sprayed her; twice Fagin's bullets struck knots or other hard-surfaced objects in the beams above her head and were deflected downward into the farther wall.

Until long after dark Fagin kept up a desultory firing, although there came no answer to his shots nor any protest of any kind.

Grace grimly endured the danger, lying there staring, as long as the light lasted, at the ceiling where the bullets struck. After darkness came she closed her eyes and listened. She spent considerable time counting the approximate number of seconds between shots, and when they ceased she found herself strangely wearied—in fact, exhausted.

Some time between the falling of darkness and midnight she heard Fagin ascending the stairs. This time he moved cautiously, but she had no difficulty in hearing him. And when he called to her through the door she did not answer, for a cold rage had seized her and she determined upon reprisal.

A dozen times Fagin called, with intervals of silence between. At last there came a silence which lasted longer than the previous ones, and then the door creaked as if Fagin had placed a shoulder against it and was trying its strength.

Still Grace remained quiet. She wanted to convince Fagin that one of his bullets had struck her.

For a while she heard him fumbling at the door, and when she decided that he was standing directly behind it she slipped her rifle around, aimed it at the center of the door, and pulled the trigger.

Instantly she threw herself back on the bed, and cringed there.

Fagin was raging, cursing, blaspheming, and by that sign she knew her bullet had struck him. Then in the hallway Fagin's heavy revolver roared, and splinters from the door flew about the room.

She was out of the line of fire, however, and in no danger except from the flying splinters. And when Fagin had emptied the contents of his revolver she laughed at him.

From beyond the door she heard his muttered maledictions, his dire threats. But she knew that as long as she could stay awake and keep herself from getting in the way of one of his bullets he could not harm her.

# CHAPTER EIGHTEEN

When Ben Gadd and Hale Seaton reached
Deming on the third day after their departure
from the Circle Dot, Seaton left Gadd to
make his purchases while he hunted up Jim
Callahan.

Seaton had said nothing to Gadd about his
intention to have a talk with the sheriff, for he
suspected that Gadd would have advised
against it. In fact, several times during the
trip to town Gadd had expressed himself as
hoping that Callahan would not hear of the
killing of his deputy, Logan, until Nevins had
got safely out of the sheriff's jurisdiction.

But Seaton felt differently. Convinced that
Nevins was innocent of the killing of Watt
Hamlin, he was prepared to argue with
Callahan on the question of sending a man
like Logan to arrest a peaceable and honest
man.

He found the sheriff in the latter's house,
in a small front room which he used as an
office. Callahan was a man of middle age,
rather short, but well built and active. He was
keen of eye and aggressive-looking. There
were genial lines about his eyes, although his
lips were thin and sternly set.

'Come in!' he said, as Seaton appeared in
the open doorway. 'I reckon I've seen you

before. You're the man who came here with that Pendleton girl, ain't you? You rode over to the Circle Dot with Ross Nevins?'

Seaton acknowledged himself identified.

'Anything I can do for you?'

'Yes,' answered Seaton.

'If it's to do with not arresting the killer Ross Nevins, I can't help you.'

'That's why I can't understand why you sent a man like Logan to arrest Nevins,' said Seaton.

Callahan opened his mouth as he shot a quick, searching glance at Seaton. Then he closed his mouth.

'H'm,' he said. 'Well,' he added, squinting his eyes at Seaton, 'you're doin' the talkin'. Why shouldn't I send a man like Logan to arrest Nevins? Can you tell me?'

'You knew Logan was a gunfighter,' said Seaton. 'And yet, being a friend of Nevins, you sent Logan after him. Therefore you are largely to blame for what happened.'

'What did happen?' asked Callahan steadily.

'Very little, from my point of view,' declared Seaton. 'When Logan tried to arrest Nevins, Nevins killed him.'

'H'm!' exclaimed Callahan. He kept his eyes on Seaton through a short silence. Then: 'Did you happen to hear Logan mention why he wanted to arrest Nevins?'

'Certainly. He said you wanted Nevins for

185

the murder of Watt Hamlin.'

'Start at the beginning an' tell me just what happened,' commanded the sheriff. His voice had changed: he was brisk, serious.

Seaton related everything that had occurred from the time he, Miss Pendleton, and Nevins had left Deming on the trip to the Circle Dot until he had seen Nevins riding away, to leave the country. For a moment after the recital the sheriff sat quiet, watching Seaton's face.

'So Ross has lit out?' he said. 'Why didn't the damned fool ride over here to see me after he'd downed Logan? He might have known that if I'd have wanted him I'd have gone after him myself.'

'You mean you haven't wanted him?' asked Seaton.

'Not any!' declared Callahan. 'Right now is the first time I've heard anything about Hamlin's bein' murdered, or about Logan tryin' to bring Nevins in. Hell, man! I don't even know Logan! I never heard of him!'

He got up and tightened his cartridge belt.

'This thing will bear lookin' into, I reckon. Seems to me there's some shenanigan goin' on. I heard about them Indians bein' on the warpath. A guy named Bell rode in here an' told how he'd seen a couple of dead Indians in a cañon north of Buckner's Flat. An' there was some soldiers over here from Fort Bayard lookin' around. There'd been a small party

186

left the reservation, they said. Not a damned one of them had come back.'

He smiled at Seaton.

'Seems with all these things goin' on, you an' Gadd hadn't ought to have left them women alone at the Circle Dot, with the outfit away. I'm gettin' a bunch together right now. We'll ride over an' see what's goin' on.'

Callahan grabbed his hat, clapped it on his head, and strode out of the office.

Seaton watched him go; then he stepped into the street, and soon found Ben Gadd in a store. He told Gadd of his talk with the sheriff, and the latter's face whitened with rage.

'Damn them scum!' he raged. 'They have framed up on Nevins!'

Gadd rushed out of the store, Seaton running after him. Gadd made his way to the livery stable and told the proprietor he wanted two of the fastest horses in the place. He raced about, helping to saddle the animals; then leaped upon one of them and plunged away, racing down the street in a cloud of dust.

Seaton followed, but had to ride several miles out into the country north of Deming before he got within hailing distance of Gadd.

They rode hard all day, and when night came they were more than halfway to the Circle Dot. Neither man said anything about halting; a camp was not to be thought of.

They rode through the night, although less rapidly than during the day, and when the dawn came they were at the crest of an upland about five miles from the ranch house.

But Gadd's horse had slowed down.

'Crow bait!' growled Gadd. 'When I get back to town I'll salivate that damned fool for givin' me a hoss like this. I'm figgerin' on shootin' him an makin' a run for it.'

Seaton did not answer. He began to pull away from Gadd, and Gadd shouted at him. 'If there's any of that scum there, you won't amount to a damn!' he yelled. 'If you ain't got sense enough to let me have your hoss, take this here gun.'

He drew his revolver and held it up to Seaton. The latter did not even look around, and Gadd grumbled profanely as the gap between them widened.

But Gadd did well, considering the condition of his horse. When he reached the level surrounding the ranch house he heard shots from somewhere in the vicinity of buildings. Seaton had vanished between two of the buildings, near the house.

Gadd used spurs and quirt and succeeded in forcing the animal under him to greater speed. But when he reached a corner of the ranch house he heard no more shots.

A sinister silence reigned.

Gadd slid off the spent horse at the edge of the front porch and ran into the house. There was no one downstairs, and he ran upstairs and opened the doors of the rooms that led off the hall, finally reaching one which was locked.

He pounded heavily, and Grace's voice reached him.

'Who is there?' she asked.

'It's Ben Gadd,' he answered.

The door opened, and Gadd found Grace's arms around his neck. As quickly as he had been hugged he was released and dragged to the window of the room Grace had occupied, where he stood with her, grinning with grim satisfaction upon beholding what was occurring on the level below.

Seaton had evidently just knocked Fagin down. For Fagin was lying flat on his back, his arms outflung. He was motionless, his eyes were closed. Lying on the ground near Fagin was a rifle. At his feet was his revolver.

Gadd was swearing softly, muttering a profane eulogy upon Seaton's prowess. At the same time he was listening to what Grace was telling him.

'And he was still shooting at me when you came,' she was saying. 'I heard Seaton's horse coming around a corner of the house, and I heard Fagin shout. Then I looked out and saw Fagin standing right down there. He had evidently emptied his rifle, for when I looked at him he was reloading.

'He tried to use the rifle on Seaton, but

Seaton rode at him so fast he had no time. He jumped sidewise and drew his revolver. But as he tried to draw it he stumbled. Before he could straighten up Seaton reached him.

'He knocked Fagin down, just as you hammered on the door. Ben,' she added, awe and admiration in her voice, 'it was a terrible blow!'

Gadd moistened his lips and grinned widely.

'Hope he's bruck the damned fool's neck!' he growled.

But Fagin's neck had not been broken, for while Grace and Gadd watched, he began to get up. Once he regained his feet, he stood swaying from side to side, throwing up his left arm as if to fend off an expected blow.

And the blow came. In spite of the upraised arm, Seaton again struck. The blow landed upon Fagin's jaw, and the man sank to his knees as though he had been struck on the top of the head with a hammer. For an instant he rested upon hands and knees, his lips drooling blood, and then he pitched forward upon his face.

Once more he struggled to his feet, and again he went down. This time he fell sidewise, striking the ground upon a shoulder. He did not move after he fell.

Gadd discovered that Grace was gripping his right arm with both hands. She was pulling at him, and her face was white and drawn.

'Oh! Oh!' she exclaimed. 'Please stop him, Ben! I am sure he will kill Fagin!'

'Huh?' ejaculated Gadd. 'I hope he does!'

But he went downstairs with Grace, and when they reached the spot where Fagin lay, the man was still motionless.

Gadd walked to him and stood grinning maliciously at the macerated face while he listened to Grace reciting to Seaton the story of her adventure. Reaction from the nervous strain was affecting the girl, and she stood, alternately laughing and crying, with her head on Seaton's shoulder, and with Seaton's arm around her.

Gadd's eyes kindled, but he said nothing. He turned away, strode to the corral, where he roped a horse, got his own saddle and bridle from a lean-to, and put them upon the animal. Then he mounted and rode to where he had left Seaton, Grace, and Fagin.

Fagin was lying on the ground near where he had fallen. He was on his back, and his hands and feet were lashed together with hogging ropes. The blood and dust on his face gave him a gruesome appearance, and his eyes were gleaming with hatred as he watched Grace and Seaton, who were standing near him.

'That's right!' declared Gadd. 'Keep him tied up. An' yet, if you'd ask me, I'd say put the cuss out of his misery! Anyway, don't let him get away until I get back. I'm ridin' to camp to get the boys. An' when we get back we're goin' to bust into that Travis bunch like you busted into Fagin!'

He wheeled his horse and sent him bounding eastward.

## CHAPTER NINETEEN

Late in the afternoon Sheriff Callahan and a half-dozen men he had sworn in as deputies arrived at the Circle Dot. While Callahan questioned Grace and Seaton and listened attentively to the girl as she related what she had overheard while standing near the stable door, the men of the posse quartered themselves in the bunkhouse.

'So Travis is that kind of a man!' said Callahan when Grace had concluded. 'Somehow, Travis never seemed to ring true to me. Too cussed swell-headed to suit me. Seems to sort of be a case for the soldiers—at least that much of it which deals with the Indians an' the Porters. But the soldiers ain't got anything to do with Watt Hamlin bein' murdered or with Travis chasin' Miss Pendleton around like he is. An' so I reckon we'll hop over to Travis's place an' have a talk with him!'

But he didn't 'hop' immediately. He and

his men had ridden hard from Deming, and darkness had come before they mounted and rode the trail taken by Edna Pendleton some days before.

Callahan was in no pleasant mood. He liked Nevins. He was mentally reviewing that conversation as he and his men rode through the night. He was conscious of a deep disappointment over Nevins's actions. It appeared that Nevins had lost confidence in him, that he had placed no trust in the friendship which had existed between them. He was a trifle irritated by the way Nevins had acted.

But his irritation toward Judge Travis was greater, and as he rode and reflected upon Travis's overbearing manner and arrogance the irritation became contempt. If he could find Travis he would arrest him and put him in jail until the occurrences of the last few days were cleared up.

He and his men rode steadily until midnight, when they reached Willets. Callahan dismounted at the front porch of the Travis house and knocked at the door, while the men of his posse silently sat in their saddles in the darkness beyond the porch.

The sheriff's knock was answered by the thin-faced woman who had responded to Edna Pendleton's summons, and she informed Callahan that the judge was not at home.

'He ain't been here for three or four days,' she said.

Callahan pushed past her and searched the house. He emerged from the front door shortly and climbed into the saddle. Followed by his men, he rode farther westward, to a level beyond the outskirts of town, where he halted.

'Travis ain't been home for three days,' he told his men. 'It's likely he's out lookin' for the Pendleton girl. Or else he's got her an' has hid her at some place. Now, it comes to this. I've got word that Travis has got about fifty men he can depend on. Some of them is meaner than poison. I've been suspectin' them.

'Travis is guilty of plannin' murder. The Pendleton girl is the only evidence against him, an' he'll try to keep her from talkin'. It's likely, if he can't do anything else with her, he'll kill her. Boys, we've got to stop that!

'But we ain't goin' to have any picnic doin' it. Looks to me like there'll have to be a cleanup. An' if there's any of you boys want back out, now is the time to do your talkin'.'

'If you're thinkin' we're that kind of men—' began one.

'Barclay, you know better than that!' gruffly said Callahan. 'I'm just clearin' myself. I don't want you boys to think I'm orderin' you to do anything. But if you're all dead set on stickin', we'll all be movin'. It ain't likely that Travis an' his bunch will do a lot of meetin' at the old Rignal shack, an' so we'll comb the country between there an' the Circle Dot an' Deming. There's any one of a half-dozen things might have happened.

'The Pendleton girl might have got away clean an' hid herself. She might have got hurt. She might have lit out somewheres with the guy that Talfer thinks met her at the Rignal place. The man Talfer told Fagin about might have been Nevins. In that case I'm bettin' there ain't a hell of a lot of harm come to the Pendleton girl.

'Or, right now Travis an' his bunch might have Nevins an' the girl cornered. We've got to bust up an' comb the country till we hit a trail.

'I'm thinkin' the Pendleton girl didn't get very far. I've told you how Travis set Naylor after her. Well, mebbe the guy that killed Naylor might have been one of the Travis gang. It might have been Travis himself. There's no tellin'.'

There on the level outside of Willets Callahan laid his plans for his search for Edna Pendleton. The task of finding and arresting Travis was one that he reserved for himself.

After giving instructions that the first man who got a clue to the whereabouts of the girl or Travis was to ride immediately to the Circle Dot, and that at the end of a week all were to meet there whether their search was

195

successful or not, Callahan sent his men scurrying out into the darkness.

★     ★     ★

Callahan himself rode back into Willets and spent the night in the vicinity of the Travis home, watching the place. He had a suspicion that the thin-faced woman had lied to him. But he detected no sign of life or movement in the house during the night, nor did Travis return.

At dawn the sheriff rode northward into the hills. He found a grass plot in a little flat rimmed by high ridges and turned his horse loose to graze, while he climbed to the crest of one of the hills where he could watch the trails leading to Willets.

On the crest of the hill, screened from the blighting rays of the sun by dense brush, he spent the greater part of the day watching Travis's house. Several times he saw the thin-faced woman; but when the dusk began to fall and he had seen no sign of Travis, he began to believe the woman had told him the truth.

He slept in the brush on the crest of the hill, and just before dawn he mounted his horse and rode eastward. He kept to the hills until he was certain that he could no longer be seen from Willets; then he rode out of them and swung into the trail leading toward the

Circle Dot, which was the trail Edna Pendleton had traveled when leaving Willets after her interview with Judge Travis.

Callahan now meant to have a look at the Rignal cabin. He knew its location, and he was familiar with the country in the vicinity.

He expected no attempt at violence from any of the Travis men he might meet. Often, when in search of a culprit or a fugitive, the sheriff rode alone, and since neither Travis nor his man knew the nature of his present errand, they could not suspect that he was searching for Travis.

About mid-morning he came in sight of the Rignal cabin. He rode boldly toward it, and when he brought his horse to a halt at the edge of the little front porch he called sharply.

There came no answer to his summons, and so he dismounted, trailed the reins over the head of his horse, crossed the little porch, and opened the door.

There was no one inside the cabin. Callahan walked to the doorway connecting the two rooms and stood for some time gazing about him. It appeared to him that no one had occupied the rooms since Edna Pendleton had been there.

And there were signs which indicated that Talfer had told the truth when he informed Fagin—according to Grace Rignal's story— that someone had been wounded during the

197

Pendleton girl's occupancy of the cabin.

But that fact did not necessarily indicate that the wounded person had been a man, as Talfer had seemed to think. The girl might have been hurt while fighting Naylor, which she would very likely do, if she had found an opportunity. As a matter of fact, it might have been Edna Pendleton herself who had killed Naylor!

The sheriff examined the wash basin he found in the front room. Blood had dried upon it, and there were, as Talfer had said, pieces of blood-soaked cloth on the floor. He went outside and found the spot under the window where Naylor had fallen. He could plainly see the imprint of the man's knees, and there was a dark stain on the sand under the window.

Callahan mounted his horse and rode a little distance westward until he reached the box cañon mentioned by Talfer in his talk with Fagin, which Grace Rignal had overheard. He saw a place where a man had camped, where a horse had left signs of a protracted stay.

He kicked around in the tall grass of the cañon and discovered a piece of blood-stained cloth, grey woolen cloth. It had been cut from the sleeve of a man's shirt, and Callahan was certain a seam at its edge was where the cuff had joined it.

He was aware that Nevins habitually wore

grey woolen shirts, and he knew that Nevins had ridden in this direction after leaving the Circle Dot. Also, Nevins had killed Logan in a gunfight, and from what he had heard of Logan he felt that the man had not been killed without first using his gun. In fact, Grace Rignal had described the fight to him, and he was convinced that Nevins had been hit.

A few minutes later, while still kicking the grass near the spot where he had found signs of a camp, Callahan stooped and picked up a small black leather tobacco-pouch. And when, upon turning the pouch over, he observed the initials 'R.M.N.' neatly branded upon the leather, his face whitened a little.

Nevins had been here! Nevins was wounded! Nevins had killed Naylor and had ridden away with the Pendleton girl!

So Callahan reasoned. The paleness of his face was that of rage at the thought that his friend, wounded, was being hounded by Travis and his men. For a time he stood staring at the tobacco-pouch. The muscles of his face and neck were corded.

But he knew that it would be futile for him to go racing about the country searching for Nevins. Nevins knew the country, and if he were hiding he would choose a place that Travis and his men would not readily find. And if he was not too badly wounded he would make any attempt to capture him a hazardous undertaking for Travis and his confederates.

Also, conceding that Travis might capture Nevins and the girl, he would not take them to Willets. According to the story Talfer had told Fagin, Travis had hinted that he would kill the Pendleton girl rather than permit her to go free to tell what she had overheard. But Callahan doubted that Travis would murder the girl. For one thing, Travis liked women rather too well to kill them.

The sheriff felt that if Travis captured the girl he would bring her to the Rignal cabin. He'd make an effort to win her, to swear her to silence, or to convince her that she had misunderstood the conversation she had overheard. Killing her would be a desperate alternative.

Callahan's men would search the country for Travis and the girl. If they found Nevins wounded, they would help him, and later they would report to Callahan at the Circle Dot. He had told them he would personally attend to anyone who might come to the Rignal cabin.

Therefore he decided to stay in the vicinity until Travis or some of his men came.

He rode back to the cabin, unsaddled, carried saddle and bridle into the old ramshackle stable on the place, and turned his horse into the tumble-down corral. Then he went into the house, sought a comfortable chair, filled his pipe, and smoked.

During the days following he made no secret of his occupancy of the cabin. He whistled, sang, and walked about. There were few provisions in the cabin, and the first day of his stay exhausted his supply of jerked beef and biscuit. So on the second day he stalked a quail and broiled it for his supper. The next day he shot a sage hen. He fared well.

He did not stay close to the cabin. On the third morning he rode a circle around it at a radius of several miles. He kept to the high country as much as possible, searching for signs of riders. Twice, eastward, he thought he observed moving dots on the skyline, and once he rode hard toward one of them, but lost sight of it.

For six days he held possession of the Rignal cabin, and he was beginning to feel that in some way Travis had received news of his presence and was avoiding the place, when on the morning of the seventh day, while he was building a fire in the stove in the kitchen, he heard the beating of hoofs outside the cabin.

He left the stove and went into the other room, where he dropped into a chair. He filled and lit his pipe, and sat there smoking as the hoof-beats came nearer. And when, looking out through one of the windows, he saw that the approaching horseman was Travis, he stealthily turned his body so that the butt of his gun was within easy reach of his right hand.

He heard Travis cross the porch, but not until Travis had been in the doorway for several seconds did he turn. Then he grinned mildly at the other.

'Howdy, Judge!' he said quietly.

Apparently Callahan's eyes were glowing with cordiality, but in reality he was keenly scrutinizing the judge's face for indications of mental disturbance. But Judge Travis's face was as lacking in signs of mental disturbance as his own.

'He's slick!' was Callahan's thought. 'That's always the way with his kind. They can be so damned crooked they can't lay straight in bed an' nobody'd suspect it. I reckon that's why they're able to do murder an' get away with it.'

'Callahan, by thunder!' exclaimed the judge.

He was not pretending his astonishment, thought the sheriff. Or if he was, he was making a good job of it. His smile was as broad and expansive as when one met him on the street in Deming. Callahan wondered if he had been home to learn from the thin-faced woman of the official visit that had been paid him by the law's representative.

'Making yourself at home, I see,' said the judge. He walked past Callahan and dropped into another chair, which he screwed around so that he was facing the sheriff. 'You're rather out of your usual haunts here, aren't you, Sheriff?'

'Some,' conceded Callahan. 'Hoss thief.'

'Come this way?'

'I reckon.'

'Whose horse?'

'Bill Wingle's.'

The judge rolled a cigarette, lit it, and smoked.

'Thought I saw a couple of strangers nosing around the country,' said he. 'Your men?'

'Uh-huh.' Callahan squinted his eyes at the judge.

'Sort of roamin' yourself, ain't you?' he remarked.

Travis's eyelashes flickered quickly. That was all the evidence he gave of emotion over the sheriff's question, but Callahan observed it.

'Nothing unusual,' he replied steadily. 'I ride. Habit of the old days.'

'That's so,' said Callahan. 'Sort of forgot you used to be a cow-puncher.' He puffed on his pipe three times during the silence that followed his words. Then he asked casually: 'Been in Deming lately?'

'Not in more than a week.'

'No court, eh? Well, things have been sort of quiet. Been home takin' it easy, I reckon?'

'Yes,' lied Travis.

'Heard anything of the Indian disturbance?' asked Callahan.

'Yes,' answered Travis. 'Too bad. I've appointed a guardian for Nellie.' He moistened his lips. 'Are the soldiers after the Indians?'

'Uh-huh. But there ain't any work for the soldiers to do, except to make a report. The war party was wiped out.'

'That's good!' declared Travis. 'Who did it?'

'That don't seem to be known. There ain't been anybody steppin' forward to take the honors. Indians was found scattered all over the flat around the Porter cabin. There was three found in a gully this side of Buckner's Flat. The major thinks it's mighty odd.'

Travis smiled. 'The soldiers ought to feel grateful,' he said.

'Uh-huh. Mebbe they are.' He looked at Travis steadily. 'Any trouble around here?' he asked.

'Not that I know of.'

'Thought there was.' Callahan pointed to the blood-stained tin wash basin on the floor near him. 'Looked to me like someone had been hurt. There's them pieces of cloth layin' around. An' right outside that window I saw a place where some one had dropped an' lost some blood. Right below that window, there!'

He pointed. Travis followed his gaze. And when Travis again faced Callahan, smiling, he was looking straight into the muzzle of the sheriff's pistol. And Callahan, grinning coldly, stood up.

'I reckon that ends this nonsense, Travis,' he said shortly. 'I'm arrestin' you for agitatin' the Indian uprisin', for bein' implicated in the massacre of the Porter family, an' for bein' behind the killin' of Watt Hamlin!'

Travis sat perfectly still. The color had gone out of his face. He drew a slow, full breath. Then his color began to return; his eyes gleamed with cold humor.

'Well, Callahan,' he complimented, 'you pulled it off rather well. At first you pretty near fooled me. I thought you were telling the truth about coming here looking for a horse thief. I was hoping you were.'

'Naturally,' said the sheriff. 'A man that's been posin' as a simon-pure limb of the law don't like to be exposed as a thief and a murderer.'

Travis laughed.

'I wasn't worrying about myself, Callahan,' said Travis softly. 'It was about you. I didn't want to have to put you out of the way for knowing too much.'

He observed Callahan's quick start of surprise, grinned broadly as he perceived the sheriff's muscles begin to stiffen.

'Don't move, Callahan!' he warned, 'and don't let your gun off!' He laughed again, mockingly.

'We've been watching you for the last two

days,' he went on. 'King, the man who is standing in the doorway with his gun on you, and myself. Drop your gun!'

Callahan smiled.

'It don't go, Travis. I've been too long in this game to go to lookin' around when I've got my man in front of me.'

He hadn't turned his head the quarter of an inch. And yet he knew Travis was telling him the truth, that there was a man standing in the doorway. He had heard a sound from the doorway, he had seen an almost imperceptible shadow on the floor at his feet. He knew he was between two fires, that he was helpless. Undoubtedly he could kill Travis. But the instant his own gun went off the man behind him would shoot.

Travis observed the indecision in his eyes.

'You know, eh?' he mocked. 'Well, perhaps we won't kill you after all, if you'll agree to some things. Toss your gun over in that corner!'

Callahan raised his arm to obey. But before his fingers relaxed their grip on the butt of the weapon there came a spiteful crash from the window on the north side of the room, and a surprised and pained grunt from the man in the doorway. The man pitched forward into Callahan, knocking him off his balance. He reeled across the room and struck the wall with a crash. The gun fell from his hand.

But while staggering from the effects of the

shock of the man lunging against him Callahan had flashed a glance out the window through which the shot had come, and had caught a glimpse of the face of one of his deputies as the latter vanished, evidently intent upon entering the room.

Callahan threw himself at his gun, which had slid into a corner. It was a convulsive leap, for he expected each instant to feel a bullet from Travis's gun; when he finally grasped his own and wheeled to face Travis, he was sitting on the floor in a corner.

But Travis had vanished. In the room was the man who had stood in the doorway. He was lying on his stomach, his face against the board of the floor, his arms flung wide, his body limp. His gun was lying just beyond his reach. Callahan knew he would never use it again.

In the doorway now stood Callahan's deputy. There was upon his lips the cold, smirking grin of the man who has killed and who is exulting in the deed.

'Got him plumb center, Jim!' he said. 'Me an' Ed was nosin' around here an' we saw Travis an' this here hombre ride up. Ed's back in the cañon.'

Callahan was not listening. In his eagerness to get upon his feet he fell again. And when he finally got up and rushed to the north window he saw Travis riding furiously northward.

With the deputy following, he ran outside. His horse was in the little corral, and his saddle and bridle in the stable. As he ran toward the corral to get his own horse he observed the atrocity which had been brought upon the animal his deputy had ridden. The unfortunate beast was lying on its side, groaning.

Callahan's lips whitened; running toward the corral, he heard his deputy blaspheming. The sheriff swore bitterly to himself. He roped his horse, saddled and bridled it, and rode to where the deputy was standing beside the injured animal. The man's face was working with passion.

'The damned skunk!' he cursed. 'A man that will do that to a hoss to save his own worthless hide ain't fit to be fed to the buzzards!' The light in his eyes was maniacal. His face was ghastly. Callahan had to speak to him three times before the deputy heard him.

'Listen, Breen,' he said. 'You ride with Ed until you meet up with some of the other boys. Then have someone hit the east trail toward the Circle Dot after more men. We're goin' to need them. Travis knows I've got the goods on him, and he'll probably light out for the hills. If I miss him I'll wait for you and Ed in that gully just this side of the Sawtooth!'

Breen nodded. When Callahan wheeled his horse and sent him thundering northward,

Breen was drawing his gun. Callahan settled himself in the saddle and thundered onward, keeping his gaze upon a moving dot in a dust cloud far ahead.

## CHAPTER TWENTY

Nevins was not in the cave when Edna awakened the next morning, and from her bunk on the ledge she saw a small fire blazing in the rock recess which Svenson had built. The aroma of steaming coffee reached her.

She had not taken her clothes off since she had occupied the cave, and so she descended the ladder, washed her face and hands and combed her hair by running her fingers through it until, she felt, it was as free from snarls as she could get it. She was coiling it into mysterious loops, and patting it and sticking hairpins into it, when Nevins came through the passageway.

He halted at the gateway and smiled at her. She moved toward him, blushing.

'I am well again,' he said. 'I am goin' out. I hope to find Travis. But first I am goin' to the Circle Dot to get the boys of the outfit. There are twenty-six of them, and they are all loyal to me. Travis would need a hundred men, instead of the fifty he boasts about, to stop them if they thought I needed them.

'We will ride back here to take you away. I won't risk letting you go with me right now, because it's pretty near certain that Travis will have a bunch of his men watching all the trails. He must know that you haven't gone very far. You will be safe here until I get back, which won't be more than three or four hours—if I find the boys at the ranch.'

'You are going to give youself up to Callahan?' she asked steadily, although her face was pale and her eyes wistful.

'After I find Travis,' he said. 'You wouldn't be safe with him alive.'

'Oh!' she said, 'why are there men like Travis?'

'Well,' he answered gravely, 'there are.'

'You are not afraid to stay here?' he asked. 'You've been mighty brave.'

'No,' she said abstractedly, for she was thinking of the danger he intended to face, and not of her own. 'No,' she repeated, 'but you—you will be careful, won't you?'

He smiled with grave reassurance.

'You don't want to get to havin' thoughts like that,' he said. 'I'll come back.'

After he had saddled and bridled his horse and the animal stood on the little level, waiting—she made him climb with her to the cleft in the towering south wall above the level. And there, with the brush screening them, they saw a number of horsemen on the vast level outside.

At first she had seen nothing to disturb her. It was not until she looked at Nevins and observed that his lips were in straight lines, that she again scrutinized the level below, to exclaim sharply.

To the southward, and apparently not more than a mile or two distant, was a group of horsemen. They were riding straight toward this place. There were perhaps thirty of the riders. Edna was certain they had seen Nevins and herself, and she crouched back against the ragged wall, trembling.

'No,' assured Nevins, 'they don't see us. They are headin' this way to intercept the two riders who are racin' in this direction from the timber. That's where the Rignal place is. Somethin' must have happened there. There's been trouble. That rider away off there is chasin' the one who is headin' for that bunch which is racin' to meet him!'

Nevins shaded his eyes with his hands and peered long at the two horsemen approaching from the direction of the timber he had mentioned. Alternately watching Nevins and the horsemen, Edna saw his eyes gleam with recognition.

'That man chasin' the other is Callahan,' he announced confidently. 'It's Callahan's horse. A big black, with a patch of white on his right hip. There ain't another horse like it in the country. The first man is Travis. I'd know that rangy brown horse anywhere.

211

'What would Callahan be after Travis for?' he queried, as though speaking to himself. 'He wouldn't know about what Travis has done, unless some of that war party got back an' the soldiers questioned them. An' even then it would be the soldiers, an' not Callahan, that would come after Travis.

'But Callahan ain't goin' to catch Travis right now!' he declared. 'That's certain. Travis is reachin' his gang. It's his gang, because they're beginnin' to open up on Callahan with their rifles!

'Shucks! They've got him!'

At a distance of perhaps a mile Callahan had slid off his horse immediately following a series of rifle reports that faintly reached the ears of the two watchers. They saw white wisps of smoke floating lazily upward from the group of riders with which Travis and his horse had merged. The group had halted.

But almost instantly, from a spot near where Callahan had slipped from his horse, there came a white puff of smoke accompanied by a faint detonation, and one of the riders in the group into which Travis had vanished threw up his arms and plunged out of the saddle.

'Callahan is needin' help,' Nevins said. 'I'm goin' down there! You stay right there!' he advised. 'If anything goes wrong, you wait until Travis's bunch has cleared out and try to reach the Circle Dot!'

He waved to her, leaped into the saddle, and raced his horse across the little level to a narrow draw that led downward along the precipitous trail.

White-lipped, concern for Nevins's safety glowing in her eyes as she began to realize she really didn't hate him, she watched him as long as she could see him. And then she clasped her hands together and stood rigid, watching the plains below. Somehow, it seemed to her that there had been a prophecy of evil in his words: 'If anything goes wrong—'

## CHAPTER TWENTY-ONE

Edna knew she could not see Nevins during his descent to the plains, although after she had glanced at the horsemen grouped on the spot where they had been when Travis had joined them, and had seen that they had not moved, she could not resist trying to get another look at Nevins.

But she did not see him.

She scanned the country in the vicinity of the place where Callahan had slipped off his horse, and she could see nothing of the sheriff either. It appeared to her that he must have been injured, for no more shots came from the place where he had fallen.

But as she watched, the group of horsemen split up. They scurried like frightened rabbits in two or three directions, clouds of dust enveloping them. Looking down upon them she could see that they were seeking depressions which would conceal them from the eyes of Callahan.

She saw a dozen of them go down into a gully. She was certain of that because she observed that some of the horses slid on their haunches with a stream of dust following them. Others were halting behind low hills. A few forced their horses to lie down in shallow depressions, while they themselves stretched out on their stomachs beside them.

In the confused scattering of the riders Edna had lost sight of the big brown horse which Nevins had said belonged to Travis. Most anxiously she looked at every horse in sight, but she could not distinguish the animal.

From her elevation she could clearly discern the formation of the land below her. It was like a giant map studded with trees, dotted here and there with ranges of small hills, darkened with gullies, gashed with gorges, and splotched with green-brown weeds and grass.

Near where the group of horsemen had halted after Travis had joined them was a gorge fringed with small trees. It was shallow out that way, widening and deepening gradually toward the bases of the hills at the foot of the mountain wall upon which Edna stood. Not more than two or three hundred feet out from the base of the wall it intersected another and deeper gorge which, Edna was convinced, was the one in which she had been riding when Naylor had roped her.

For a time Edna observed no movement on the part of Travis's men. They seemed to be waiting for Callahan to show himself, for she could see that they were all facing the point from which the sheriff had sent the bullet which had killed one of their number.

But Callahan did not reveal himself. Even Edna, from her point of vantage, could not discover his whereabouts. She feared he was wounded.

But now, scanning the plains as far as her vision would permit, she was attracted by a dust cloud slowly traveling toward her from the direction of the timber which surrounded the Rignal cabin. She followed the progress of the dust cloud until she saw it reach the spot where Callahan had disappeared. And when it had come that near she saw that in the cloud were two men riding one horse.

She saw the horse come to a sliding halt, as if someone had suddenly commanded it to halt. And the animal had hardly become motionless when the two riders slid from its back, so quickly that they appeared to fall.

But she could just see them worming their way on their stomachs away from the horse, and so she suspected that Callahan was still alive, and that he had called to the men, warning them of the presence of Travis's adherents.

Edna drew a breath of relief. Callahan was not alone, anyway. The odds against him were not so great. She felt like clapping her hands with joy.

And then, far away eastward, she saw another dust cloud. This cloud was a huge one, and its enormous size indicated the presence on it of a considerable number of horsemen.

She watched the cloud for a while, observing that it was traveling in a section of low country, and that it would not be readily seen by Travis's men, concealed in their gullies, gorges, and depressions.

She had a wild hope that the riders in the dust cloud were Circle Dot men who by some magic means had learned of her predicament and were coming to help her. And when she considered that she had been absent from the Circle Dot for a number of days, and that by now Grace Rignal must be desperately trying to find her, she felt she had some foundation upon which to rest her hope.

Far away southward she now observed three other dust clouds. They, too, were headed toward her, and at first she thought they were merely miniature whirlwinds such as she had seen lazily traveling through the country. But as they came closer she perceived that they too were caused by horsemen, traveling rapidly.

Whatever elements—good or bad—the dust clouds concealed, they were all moving toward her, converging upon a point almost directly below her. And because of the presence of Callahan she felt that at least some of the approaching riders must be his friends.

She was now assailed with a queer feeling of omniscience. From her lofty retreat she could observe the movements of all the riders on the plain below her, though she knew that some of them at least could not be aware of the presence of others near them. She could be almost certain that Travis's men, concealed from Callahan and the riders in the dust clouds, could not know of the steady and rapid approach of the others. Her only concern, her really vital concern, was for the safety of Nevins.

And after a while, with the horsemen approaching from the east still a considerable distance away, she saw directly beneath her a horseman riding rapidly through a deep gorge. The gorge was the one in which Naylor had captured her. It was intersected by the smaller gorges which ran past the spot where some of Travis's men were concealed.

The horseman was Nevins.

Breathlessly she followed his movements. She observed that he halted where the small gorge intersected the large one, and paused, as though debating which way to go. She wanted to shout at him, to warn him away from the smaller gorge, but she knew that her voice would not carry to him. And so she stood motionless, tense, waiting.

When she saw Nevins ride on again, following the big gorge, she drew her breath regularly. She knew he would seek Callahan, and she followed his progress through the gorge and saw him at last reach the place where the sheriff had dismounted from his horse and where, later, he had been joined by the two other men.

For a while nothing happened. The three dust-clouds which had been approaching from the south presently disclosed horsemen. These headed for the spot where the sheriff and his friends had concealed themselves. They and their horses vanished. Edna was convinced that they had sunk into a gully.

And now, except for the big body of men approaching from the east, there was no movement on the plains below. Such of Travis's men as she could still see were lying motionless in their coverts, waiting. Callahan, Nevins, and the others were not visible. The group of riders from the east came onward steadily. They were now not more than half a mile from the gorge which concealed most of Travis's men.

The country below Edna was so calm and peaceful that despite her knowledge of the sinister preparations of the men of the various factions, she was almost convinced that there would be no trouble. It did not seem possible to her that the slumberous, smiling land lying there so serenely could be inhabited by men who were eager to kill one another.

For a time she stood in the cleft of the wall, trembling with dread. And when the horsemen from the east, clattered to the crest of the slope that led to the level upon which Travis's men were waiting, and halted, she forgot to breathe.

There was an instant of dull, dead silence, during which it seemed to her that the men below her were images of dreams. The silence was so profound that her ears ached with it. And then, from some brush that fringed the eastern slope of the small gorge, there appeared a fleecy puff of smoke at the end of a slender lance of fire.

A faint report reached her ears and she saw one of the riders from the east pitch out of the saddle.

Again there was a scurrying of horses. A pall of dust obscured them for a time. And when the dust settled she could see neither men nor horses. But from dozens of places appeared fleecy puffs of smoke and thin lances of fire. A faint popping, as of miniature firecrackers being exploded intermittently, floated upward to her ears.

At first the smoke puffs came from positions which she had no trouble in defining as marking the strategic spots which Travis's men, and the riders from the east, and Callahan and his friends, had chosen. But after a while the men slowly shifted their positions. The lines of battle appeared to lengthen and broaden until the entire vast level below her was filled with little puffs of smoke.

She lost all knowledge of the whereabouts of Nevins and Callahan. There came a time when the whole expanse of level was obscured from her view by a thick, heavy cloud of white smoke which floated sluggishly to the whims of a desultory breeze, and which finally brought to her nostrils the acrid odor of burned powder. But through the smoke she could still see slender streaks of fire darting here and there like fiery serpents.

Faintly to her ears came yells of pain, shouts, curses. Through the smoke she could see plunging horses and running men. There were no fire lances from the position that Callahan and Nevins had taken, and she concluded that they had come forward, toward the center of the mêlée.

One thing she knew. It was that the eastern riders were Circle Dot men. For just as they had halted, and before she had seen the puff of smoke from the edge of the smaller gorge, she had recognized Ben Gadd. She would have known him at even a greater distance.

Once or twice during a lull in the firing the smoke lifted and thinned, and through breaches and rifts she could see the bodies of men lying on the level.

An hour passed. The firing grew spasmodic. There would come a period during which there would be no sound from below. Then would follow a series of reports. And then silence again. Half a dozen times during periods of silence a faint but vicious report would reach her. Sometimes silence would immediately follow. Often the single report would precede half a dozen which seemed to answer the first.

Once, out beyond the cloud of smoke she saw a rider thundering away, evidently intent upon escaping. He was crouched low in the saddle and was furiously plying a quirt. He got quite a little distance out into the clear atmosphere, and she was watching him intently, trying to identify him, when she observed a little puff of dust rise from his back, between the shoulders.

The rider straightened, threw up his arms, and pitched sidewise out of the saddle into a barren stretch. He lay there, his arms outflung, motionless, while the horse raced onward wildly, reins and stirrups flapping.

After a while there came another lull; long, this time. The smoke disintegrated and floated eastward in long, trailing wisps. The air grew clearer. It appeared to her that the battle must be over, and she twined her fingers nervously together and prayed aloud that Callahan and the Circle Dot men might win and that Nevins would be spared.

The tension upon her nerves had grown so great that during the interval in which she could clearly see the level upon which the fighting had been done, she felt that ages were passing while she watched.

And then she saw the level writhe with life again. Below her chaos reigned. Men and horses leaped back and forth in a confused mass. Smoke again filled the air. Explosions, louder this time, told her that the men were using revolvers.

She felt that this was the last phase of the fight. The combatants had come to close quarters, and one side or the other must win quickly. In her excitement she got to her knees in the cleft, and at the risk of falling leaned far out to get a better view of the fighting.

And then out of the mass of plunging horses went a rider. Two, three, four. They fled southward, riding as had ridden the other man who had been shot when he had tried to escape, low in their saddles, plying their quirts frenziedly.

One by one they were sent from their saddles by bullets that followed them from the fighting mass on the level. Others followed. Two or three escaped. She watched them reach a far ridge, go over it, vanish.

It was not long then until quiet again reigned. Straining her eyes toward the level, she could see men standing down there, motionless. Riderless horses were galloping about. But the fighting was over.

For a few minutes, doing her best to restrain the terrible impatience that now assailed her, she stood watching. But she could not recognize any of the men, and so she climbed down the cleft in the wall and went into the cave to wait for Nevins.

She had been in the cave only a few minutes when she found that she could no longer endure the uncertainty. She felt she must descend to the level, must make an effort to discover what had happened to Nevins.

So she ran down into the valley and caught her horse, leading him by the hackamore to the upper level upon which she had sat the night before watching the stars.

She tied the animal to a rock while she went into the cave and got her saddle. Then with shaking hands and quaking heart she stood, trying to compose herself long enough to force her trembling hands to place saddle and bridle on. She finally got them in place

223

and was just reaching for a stirrup when she heard the beating of hoofs in the little draw through which Nevins had gone.

She turned, standing beside the horse, and waited for him to appear.

But it was not Nevins who came up the draw. Judge Travis, riding the big brown horse which he had been riding when Callahan was pursuing him, appeared at the top of the draw.

And Travis, his face flaming with rage, his eyes glowing with a lust to kill, reached for the gun at his hip!

## CHAPTER TWENTY-TWO

Palsied with fear over the terrible appearance of Travis, convinced that he meant to kill her, Edna involuntarily dodged behind her horse. Travis's weapon belched fire at her just as she moved.

She had the bridle reins in her hand when Travis appeared. She had not released them when she had moved around the animal. And, frightened by the sudden appearance of Travis and his horse, and terrified by the crashing report close to his ears, the animal reared until he stood on his hind legs. And so sudden and powerful was the motion that Edna was lifted clear off the ground and swung back against the horse's flanks.

The horse wheeled as he reared, and Travis's animal, coming on with speed unchecked, rushed against him. The shock of the collision threw both horses down. Edna's horse fell almost in its tracks. But Travis's horse, with the judge on its back, toppled over at the edge of the slope and went rolling over and over down into the valley.

Edna had been thrown again. She was lying across the saddle when her horse regained its feet. Snorting with fright, it leaped down the slope, veered sharply upon nearing the judge's horse, and went plunging out into the valley with Edna clinging desperately to the saddle horn.

The animal ran more than a mile before it heeded the girl's frantic jerks on the bridle rein and slowed down. And when it finally came to a halt, facing the slope down which the judge's horse had rolled, Edna gently slid off its back into the deep grass.

A little later, when she regained consciousness and sat up, she still gripped the bridle rein, and the horse was standing beside her, grazing.

She got up, reeling dizzily, and looked about her, trying to remember what had happened. And when, over at the bottom of the slope, she saw Travis climbing into the saddle, she cried aloud in dismay.

She mounted and sent the horse racing

down the valley.

She felt that Travis and his men had lost the battle which had been fought on the plains outside the valley. When the judge had come thundering up the draw to the little level he had not worn the triumphant expression of the victor. A terrible rage and disappointment had been depicted on his face.

His action in shooting at her could mean only one thing: that he blamed her for bringing Callahan and the Circle Dot men against him, and meant to kill her so that she could not bear evidence against him when he finally stood facing the law that he had outraged.

She was recovering from the dizziness that had assailed her, and she was aware that if she was to escape Travis she must maneuvre to get him to the far end of the valley so that she could reach the entrance through which he had come and make an effort to gain the protection of the Circle Dot men, who must still be on the outside plains.

She held one advantage which she quickly used. Her horse was fresher than his, and she instantly straightened him for a trial of speed. In five minutes she was far ahead of Travis.

She reached the low mesa which she had admired from a distance, rode to its farther end, and into some brush at its base, and watched Travis. She could plainly see him, and observed that his horse was running heavily. She perceived, too, that Travis intended to trap her, if he could.

Far ahead was a narrow stretch of plain running between a mountain wall on the west side and a solemn-looking bastioned hill on the east. The mesa was shorter on the east side than upon the west, and the narrow stretch of land through which she must pass to continue her flight up the valley was some distance eastward of the mesa, so that if Travis kept going straight ahead he would travel a shorter distance to reach the narrow stretch than she, if she continued to go toward it.

She saw Travis's horse go lumbering past the southern end of the mesa. Then she rode back the way she had come, swinging wide as she reached the southerly end of the mesa, so that Travis, if he were lurking close to the wall, could not intercept her.

But he was not there, and after she cleared the mesa she glanced back, to see him racing straight ahead toward the narrow stretch of land, down the valley.

She did not halt to watch him, but kept her horse running hard toward the entrance to the valley. When she turned her head to see what had become of him, she was on the little level from which she had viewed the stars, and she was tingling with exultation over her escape, when her horse sank under her and she was thrown headlong out of the saddle.

She hadn't been hurt badly, only shaken, she told herself when she recovered consciousness to find herself lying at the edge of the slope. The breath had been knocked out of her and she sat for some time, painfully filling her lungs and running her hands over her body in search of injuries.

She found none. She sat up and looked around for her horse, to find the animal standing not more than half a dozen feet distant, looking at her.

She was glad she hadn't been unconscious very long, for that would have given Travis time to reach her. And then, with sinking heart, she realized that she must have been unconscious longer than she had thought, for not more than a hundred feet out in the valley she saw him.

Curiously, Travis was not coming toward her. He had halted his horse. Her first thought was that the animal had stopped of its own volition, exhausted. Perhaps that really was what had happened. She never discovered the reason.

But she could not mistake Travis's motions, nor his intention.

He was drawing his rifle from its saddle sheath. While she watched him, fascinated, physically unable to get to her feet because of the dismay that had seized her, and because her muscles seemed to be paralyzed from her fall, she saw him draw the weapon and fumble for an instant with the mechanism.

Then, although she was still unable to move, she saw him lift the rifle to his shoulder, and his malignant eyes glared at her over the sights. She whispered a prayer, and it seemed to be answered.

Amazed, she saw the rifle muzzle move to her right. Flame spurted from it. Behind her, a little to her right, she heard another rifle go off. She saw Travis straighten in the saddle, saw him jerk backward as though he had been struck violently in the chest. But he steadied and threw the rifle up again.

Again Edna felt the air rock from a report at her right and slightly behind her. This time Travis tumbled backward off his horse, landing flat upon his back in the tall grass and lying there motionless, while the horse, frightened, snorted and wheeled, and plunged down the valley.

Not until she saw Travis lying still on the ground did Edna turn. And then behind her, a smoking rifle in his hands, she saw Nevins. Behind him, clattering up through the draw, were a number of other men. She thought there must be twenty or thirty of them.

She recognized Gadd and Seaton. And there, too, was Callahan. The sheriff was grinning widely. He seemed to be satisfied. And away back, down the draw, she caught sight of Grace Rignal.

Then all the faces, blurred in her vision, were blotted out by a curtain of darkness that seemed to descend upon her eyes.

## CHAPTER TWENTY-THREE

To the valley where they had hidden Edna and Nevins came again a month later, when the heat of June had begun to shrivel and blight the vendure of the plains. They rode up through the draw an hour before twilight began to settle, and they found that the sun had wrought no havoc in the valley. It stretched before them, green and beautiful, as entrancing as it had been on the day Edna had first seen it, with Nevins, from the crest of the slope where later she had passed many hours alone.

The full story of the incidents which had led to the battle on the plains between Travis's men and Callahan's posse and the men of the Circle Dot had been told her. She had learned that Travis had intended to kill her because of her knowledge of his deeds. And as they came up through the draw and halted on the little level overlooking the valley, Nevins was supplying details.

'Matt Blandell confessed after he'd been shot, an' when he found he wasn't going to live much longer,' said Nevins. 'He confessed to killin' Watt Hamlin. He'd been trailin' us that day when we left Deming to ride to the Circle Dot. You'll remember I was actin' mean to you.'

She smiled at him, blushed.

'Anyway, Blandell trailed us. He was wantin' to shoot me in the back, but he got no chance. He was afraid to get close enough. He found my knife in the gorge where I had to kill the Indians. He rode to the Circle Dot, climbed in the window, and tried to hang Seaton, thinkin' he was hangin' me. Seems he had some idea that if he knifed Hamlin an' swung me, folks would think I'd killed Hamlin an' hung myself. It's mighty strange what ideas men get.'

'And what of Nellie Porter?' asked Edna.

'I'm tellin' you a secret,' he said. 'Brandt Adams was killed, too, in the fight. An' the new judge has turned Nellie over to me—an' you. If you'll agree, she'll stay with us. She'll be company, if we think we need it, after Grace goes away with Seaton.'

'So you have seen that?' she said, giving him a surprised glance.

'My eyes not having gone back on me, I have,' he answered, grinning at her. 'You see, when a man's in love he don't make a heap of effort to conceal it. He's so happy, a blind man, hearin' him near, could tell what's the matter with him.'

'Yes,' she smiled. 'I have noticed that.'

231

And then her eyes became serious. 'Do you think we will ever have any more trouble with the men Travis left? Those that got away?'

'I reckon not. They've left the country. They'll not come back. An' between you an' me, there wasn't a lot of them got away. The Circle Dot boys were pretty mad.'

'And what of Fagin?'

'Fagin! Shucks. He's headed for the Federal penitentiary. By the time he gets out he'll have all the fight taken out of him. An' there never was very much in him.'

Edna and Nevins had been married that day. A bishop, visiting at Deming, had heard their story and had been eager to accept Nevins's invitation to spend a few days at the Circle Dot. He had sent them away that afternoon with his blessing.

Nevins had told no one, not even Edna, where he intended to enjoy the days of their honeymoon. He had been gravely mysterious about his plans. It was only when he headed his horse toward the entrance to the valley that Edna had an inkling of his intentions. And ever since they had left the plains behind them she had pretended that she was ignorant of the reason for their coming here.

But now her cheeks were flaming and she would not look at him.

The vivid colored panorama of the afterglow engaged their attention for a time, as they sat on their horses watching the sky, each thinking of the time they sat together on the crest of the slope above the valley, watching the stars.

'Oh!' she exclaimed, 'isn't it beautiful!'

'The sky or the valley?' he asked, watching her.

'The valley,' she answered. 'I—I never want to leave it—for long! Do you know what I should like to do? I should like to build a house down there, right in the middle of it, where at night I could come out and see the stars! It is our valley of the stars.'

'You like it that well?' he said. His eyes were glowing. He helped her down from her horse, removed the saddles and bridles, and turned both animals loose to graze. He stood, pretending not to be aware of her astonishment, watching the horses as they scampered down the slope and cavorted in the deep grass of the valley.

He smiled and looked at Edna.

'They like it here too,' he said.

'But why did you do that?' she asked, although she knew what his answer would be. 'It will be dark very soon and we should be going—where are we going.'

'An' miss seein' the stars?' he asked. 'I have been thinkin' of this night,' he added. 'I've been wonderin' about railroad trains an' hotels and people—crowds of people. They're curious. Seems they are always searchin' for somethin' an' not findin' it.

'There's times when I like to be alone with someone I like pretty well,'—he smiled gravely at her—'so that I can sit with her and talk, sayin' a great many things that I've been kept from sayin', with no one to look at us but the stars.'

She was silent, watching him, divining the solemn thoughts which he could not find words to express. And she knew that he had set his heart upon this adventure, and she could not deny him.

'We shall stay,' she said. 'It will not be the first night we have passed here.'

'And it won't be the last!' he declared. 'For if treatin' you right will keep us together, we'll be visitin' this valley for so many years that we'll grow old countin' them.'

They stood, silent now, watching the twilight come. And just before the light faded he took her by an arm and guided her down the narrow passageway to the cave in which they had spent many hours together.

He halted in the gateway and looked at her with a smile, for she had exclaimed sharply, delightedly, at what she saw.

For the cave had been furnished to resemble a room in a house. Neatly arranged in it were various articles of furniture, draperies, a carpet, rugs, lamps.

But not for many hours were the lamps lighted. For they sat for a long time on the crest of the slope above the valley, out where they could feel the slight night breeze, where they could drink in the glowing emerald beauty of the valley, and where they could see the sea of stars, like countless eyes peering through a gauze veil of softest blue velvet, smiling at them.

Photoset, printed and bound in Great Britain by REDWOOD BURN LIMITED, Trowbridge, Wiltshire.

$$\begin{array}{r} 392 \\ 240 \\ \hline 152 \end{array}$$

22

$$\begin{array}{r} 150 \\ 150 \\ \hline 300 \end{array}$$

$$\begin{array}{r} 92 \\ 400 \\ \hline 20 \end{array}$$

$$\begin{array}{r} 812 \\ 182 \\ \hline 1994 \\ 250 \\ \hline 2234 \end{array}$$